THE BELLS OF Christmas

Book 4 of the Christmas Card Series

Amanda Tru

Published by

Olivia Kimbrell Press™

Fort Knox, KY

Copyright Notice

The Bells of Christmas: Book 4 of the Christmas Card Series

Copyright © 2022 by Amanda Tru. All rights reserved. No part of this publication may be reproduced or transmitted in any form or by any means — electronic, mechanical, photocopying, or recording — without express written permission of the author. The only exception is brief quotations in printed or broadcasted critical articles and reviews.

This book is a work of fiction. Names, characters, places, and incidents are either the product of the author's imagination or are used fictitiously. Any resemblance to actual events, organizations, places, locales or to persons, living or dead, is purely coincidental and beyond the intent of either the author or publisher. The characters are productions of the author's imagination and used fictitiously.

PUBLISHED BY: Olivia Kimbrell Press™*, P.O. Box 470, Fort Knox, KY 40121-0470. The Olivia Kimbrell Press™ colophon and open book logo are trademarks of Olivia Kimbrell Press™.

Olivia Kimbrell Press™ is a publisher offering true-to-life, meaningful fiction from a Christian worldview intended to uplift the heart and engage the mind.

Some scripture quotations courtesy of the King James Version (KJV) of the Holy Bible. Some scripture quotations courtesy of the New King James Version (NKJV) of the Holy Bible, Copyright© 1979, 1980, 1982 by Thomas-Nelson, Inc. Used by permission. All rights reserved.

Cover Art and Graphics by Danica Djurdjevic (danicadjurdjevic.com/)

Fonts: Crimson Pro, Allura, Dark Courier

Library Cataloging Data

Names: Tru, Amanda (Amanda Tru) 1978-

Title: Once Upon a Christmas; Book 3 of the Christmas Card series / Amanda Tru

    256 p. 5.5 in. × 8.5 in. (13.97 cm × 21.59 cm)

Description: Olivia Kimbrell Press™ digital eBook edition | Olivia Kimbrell Press™ Trade paperback edition | Kentucky: Olivia Kimbrell Press™, 2020.

Summary: A once upon a Christmas inspires her story. Her ever after could change the world.

Identifiers: ISBN-13: 978-1-68190-253-1 (ebk.) | 978-1-68190-254-8 (trade)

1. clean romance love story 2. women's inspirational 3. man woman relationships 4. Christian living 5. Christmas Card book 6. based on a true story 7. holiday season couple

Book 4 of the Christmas Card Series

Amanda Tru

Table of Contents

The Bells of Christmas 1
   Copyright Notice ii
Table of Contents v
Dedication: vii
Chapter 1 1
Chapter 2 9
Chapter 3 21
Chapter 4 35
Chapter 5 49
Chapter 6 57
Chapter 7 77
.... 85

Chapter 8	87
Chapter 9	95
Chapter 10	109
Chapter 11	125
Chapter 12	131
Chapter 13	151
Chapter 14	165
Chapter 15	177
Chapter 16	189
Chapter 17	201
Chapter 18	211
Epilogue	231
Personal Note	233
Share Your Thoughts	237
Readers Guide	239
More Books:	243
About Amanda Tru	245

To all of you waiting in silence,
hoping someone will hear the bells.
Listen.
I'm ringing them for you.

Chapter One

Tayde paused in front of the sterile, gray door. She breathed in. And out.

This was it. The work of her entire adult life culminated in the next few ticks of the clock. This was the moment her life would change.

With one last deep breath, she raised her fist and knocked twice on the door.

"Come." The answer came immediately. It wasn't friendly, but neither was it harsh. Businesslike—exactly as it should be.

Tayde twisted the knob and opened the door, noting the absence of the door's usual protesting squeak. The office's new occupant was already attending to all the details under her purview, even the squeaks.

Tayde stepped into the office, taking the space in with a quick glance. The room was empty except for a desk with a computer and a few other office supplies scattered across the surface. Tayde couldn't tell if her new boss hadn't yet had a chance to decorate or if the stark, gray walls and emptiness *was* the décor.

There wasn't even a chair across from the desk. Was she just supposed to stand? And if so, where?

Parking herself three feet in front of the desk, Tayde started, "Hi, Ms. Sutton, I'm—"

"I just emailed you your new assignment." Sheryl Sutton's gaze remained on the computer screen, not sparing even a sideways glance in Tayde's direction. "It's a regular column that we will use as material for online advertising. Can you handle that?"

Tayde's breath caught, thrilled yet startled. Tayde had never met her new boss before, and she didn't know that this would count as an actual "meeting" either. The dark-haired woman in her early fifties still didn't bother with a glance at the person her curt words addressed.

In the span of a half second, Tayde mentally worked to shift her expectations from everything she'd thought this meeting would entail to the reality before her.

"Yes," she said in a rush, afraid her dream would disappear like a mirage before her brain could tell her hand to grab it and hang on tight. A regular column at a respected magazine was what she'd wanted. It was happening. She was going to be a legitimate writer.

"I sent you the material in a folder labeled 'Viewer Letters.' I will update the folder as more come in. It's essentially a 'Dear Abby' column where you take a complaint, validate it, and respond with your own clever commentary. You're giving a microphone to the wrongs of the world and offering frivolous advice on how society should right them. Or, in your case, the right is spelled with a 'w.' That's why the column is titled *Wrongs Made Wright*."

Tayde's excitement deflated like a full balloon let go by a child's fingers. Tayde needed to sit down. Really needed to sit down. But shifting back and forth between her jelly-filled legs was her only option.

"That's why you chose me for this assignment?" Tayde choked out, connecting the dots to the unavoidable conclusion. "Because of my name?"

Sheryl didn't even flinch. Instead, she turned and speared Tayde with a look that dared her to find fault. "Tayde Wright is the perfect name. I could have gone with the more experienced writers, but 'Wrongs Made Johnson' doesn't have the same ring to it. I'm taking a risk by assigning this to you." She subtly raised an eyebrow, watching Tayde's reaction.

Tayde's mouth felt dry, and she could barely get enough air to breathe, let alone speak. Though her words sounded airy, her indignation forced her to speak them anyway. "Are you putting me in charge of the complaint box?"

Sheryl laughed, but it held little humor. "Nicely put. Yes. It's a strategy. By using reader input, we include our readership in our content. Someone writes in to complain about something ridiculously wrong; we publish it and then use it on social media to drive traffic to our webpage. It's simple."

Sheryl narrowed her eyes as she turned back, focusing once again on the computer screen. Then she shook her head, the corners of her mouth curling with disgusted amusement. "You can't believe the things people do. Plenty of content here for outlandish, ridiculous news. And it comes right to our office."

Tayde's mind screamed at her to shut up. But, as usual, her mouth paid no heed. "You want me to write clickbait?"

Sheryl turned back to look at Tayde, her steely gray eyes

piercing her with startling intensity. "Yes. Yes, I do. Do you have a problem with that?"

Tayde clenched her jaw, arguing with herself over how to reply. She needed this job. This may be the only opportunity she'd have. No, it wasn't the opportunity she wanted, but what if it was the only chance she got? In her mind, she heard herself offering a meek, *No, ma'am. I don't have a problem. Thank you for the opportunity.*

But there was fire within her. She'd never been a "yes, sir" type of person. It'd been a problem in the past, but that same bold determination had gotten her here. She couldn't stop being herself. No matter if she was talking to the president of the United States, royalty, or Sheryl Sutton, she would state her mind because that's who she was.

"Not a problem," Tayde assured. "But it's not what I anticipated. I took this job to be a writer. And because of you. I wanted to work with Sheryl Sutton. But I thought this magazine was more than online clickbait. I thought I would get a chance to report, write, and learn from the best. It's not the direction I thought the magazine was going."

Sheryl's mouth puckered, but she didn't seem angry. "I was hired for one purpose—to save an old, outdated magazine. We're not a newspaper. And we're not located in New York, Washington, or L.A. to cover pop culture, politics, or entertainment. Yes, the magazine has a long history, but it's extinct in this day and age. The only option is to revamp and do something completely different that will carve a new niche for us. I'm taking the magazine online. We'll focus on human interest that appeals to a national audience. You can't make money with a print magazine and physical subscribers anymore. We have no choice but to shift our focus to court advertisers and page views. That's not what you signed up for.

I get that. But what you signed up for no longer exists."

"And why did you sign up for it?" Tayde's question startled into the silence. She kinda hated herself. But she'd come this far. Hurriedly, she rushed to explain. "You have a name as an investigative journalist. You could have a job anywhere. Why a dying magazine in Brighton Falls?"

Tayde held her breath, hoping she hadn't gone too far. She'd challenged Sheryl on the assignment. Now she was asking personal questions that technically had nothing to do with her presence in the office. It was none of her business, and she knew it.

A light sparked in Sheryl's eyes, and Tayde couldn't tell if it was annoyance, amusement, or respect. Then the older woman's gaze softened. She picked up a frame on her desk. "I'm no longer young enough for the in-depth, edge-of-the-world assignments. I don't have a youthful body and lack the energy or desire to do the tough jobs demanded in top investigative journalism. I've put in my time. But I'm not yet ready to retire. And Brighton Falls has one thing the larger cities and big-name media companies can never compete with."

She turned the frame around, revealing a picture of a man holding a toddler. "My son and grandson. I wasn't around for my son's childhood. His father raised him. I've had many adventures, but I decided what I wanted most was the adventure of my grandson."

Though Tayde had asked the question, she felt immediately uncomfortable with the answer. Sheryl was tough. She had a hard edge about her that Tayde recognized in her writing and the interviews the well-known journalist had given over the years. This glimpse of a softer side and hint of regret felt unnerving. It wasn't what Tayde had expected. She knew Sheryl had some purpose in accepting the editor position at a magazine decades past its prime. Still, Tayde had imagined grandiose reasons to launch the publication on a competitive level relevant to today's world. And Tayde hoped to hitch along for the ride to the top. She hadn't expected Sheryl Sutton to accept a position for a personal reason.

For once, Tayde didn't know what to say. Phrases floated through her mind, all sounding cheesy and none sounding appropriate. Several heartbeats passed while Tayde struggled. *That's nice,* sounded stupid. *Good for you,* sounded completely ingenuine.

Sheryl turned the picture frame back around and set it down facing her, once again hiding the faces of her son and grandson from Tayde's view.

"Now let's talk about you," she said, eliminating the need for Tayde to formulate a response.

But the intense look the older woman leveled on Tayde eliminated any relief she felt. The brief glimpse at Sheryl's softer side was now firmly shuttered, leaving a cold, harsh demeanor with no hint that warmth had or would ever exist.

"You fancy yourself a writer, but you're not." Her words came sharp and cutting, flung out at Tayde as if they were darts aimed at a target. "You are a copy editor. You possess a degree with no experience. You were desperate to break into the writing world. You were hired before my contract was finalized. I bet they threw my name around like confetti in your interview. You saw me as your big break."

Tayde tried not to show that Sheryl's words hit their mark. Each darted accusation hit a direct bullseye, creating wounds until Tayde couldn't separate the individual pain. She couldn't defend herself, not because she didn't dare stand up for herself, but because she knew Sheryl's words to be true. They were an audible echo of a refrain endlessly coursing through Tayde's mind.

You don't deserve to be here... You'll never be a writer... If they only knew what a fake you really are...

Tayde stood tall, lifted her chin, and took the continuing onslaught.

"I did not hire you," Sheryl continued coldly. "Nor would I have hired you if given a choice." Though her words were harsh, they weren't angry. "You are more than welcome to find a different job more in line with your expectations. I have other, more experienced writers. Against my better judgment, I'm giving you a chance."

"Because of my name."

"Yes."

There it was. Not platitudes. No false flattery about how Sheryl believed in her. No pep talk. Sheryl presented the situation in its stark reality and challenged Tayde to deal with it.

"Then it sounds like it's my lucky day," Tayde said firmly. "When do you need my first column?"

"End of the day tomorrow," Sheryl replied flatly. "We publish the next day. We launch our new direction immediately, and I need your column to draw in views. With the tight timeline, I chose your first complaint letter. You do a good job, and I may let you choose the next one yourself. This one is regarding the Fourth of July yesterday—another reason we need to publish while the holiday is still fresh. Everything must be live on the sixth or else it will be considered old news. At the moment, it is valid, current, and pulls on the patriotic heartstrings. It's the perfect opportunity—that is if you turn out to be a decent writer."

Tayde felt the immediate pressure. She glanced at the wall clock, noting it was already the end of the workday. That meant she had exactly twenty-four hours to write a column that would impress Sheryl and work as the quality "clickbait" needed to rescue the failing magazine and launch it into relevance. It wasn't the investigative, literary journalism she dreamed of. But a person has to eat. If you can't eat steak, sometimes you have to settle for potato chips. She needed a job, and at least she was writing, not editing, the online junk food.

Sheryl turned away from Tayde, her focus returning to her computer. Tayde knew she'd been dismissed.

"I'll get to work right away," Tayde announced before turning to leave.

She hadn't made it out the door when Sheryl's voice sent a chill through her.

"I like you, Miss Wright. Don't disappoint."

Tayde didn't stop but hurriedly retreated out the door, Sheryl's words echoing in her mind long after the gray door had shut.

Chapter Two

Tayde opened the door to her apartment and dropped her bag on the couch. She thought about trying to make it to her bedroom but decided it wasn't worth it. Instead, she plopped on the couch beside her bag and sprawled out, almost melting into the worn suede in pure exhaustion.

Less than ten seconds later, her eyes popped open in alarm.

She recognized her brother's voice, which wasn't shocking in itself. After all, he was her roommate in what Tayde felt was the perfect arrangement. She had help paying the bills, and it didn't cost her putting up with someone else's weird habits and trying to be nice about it. She'd had a lifetime to be familiar with Knox Wright's eccentricities. Though they were many, they were either tolerable or so familiar that she was moderately desensitized to them.

It was his tone. That barely concealed impatience and

aggravation mixed with a hint of eagerness to please—it was Knox's signature voice when speaking to—

"Hey, Mom! Tayde's here!" Knox's eyes lit up as soon as he stepped out of his bedroom. "You said you tried to call her earlier, but she didn't answer? Well, she's here now. Do you want to talk to her?"

Tayde's eyes flew wide in panic. She made quick jerky motions back and forth with her head, demanding he stop.

He looked at her with wide-eyed innocence.

"I've got to run anyway," he continued. "I've got a date tonight. But I'm looking at her right now. If you call, I'm sure she'll answer." He looked at Tayde, flashed a grin, and nodded eagerly.

"No!" Tayde hissed. "No, Knox! Don't! I don't want to—"

"K. Love you, Mom." He kept grinning and nodding, pretending to be oblivious to her protests. "Yes, if we need more items for the bake sale at school, I'll let you know. Yeah... uh huh... Ok... Call Tayde. Love you. Bye."

He pressed the end button on his phone. Less than a half second later, a pillow hit his hand in a direct hit from Tayde's irate launch. "Jerk! You didn't have to do that! You have no idea how exhausted I am."

Knox shrugged. "Seem to have energy enough to fire pillows at an innocent guy. I just thought you'd want some quality Mom time. I've gotta run and didn't want you to spend the evening alone."

Tayde scoffed, "Yeah, right. You didn't want 'Mom time,' so you pawned her off on me!"

Tayde's phone rang, and she whined like an upset two-year-old, "Are you seriously going out on a date now? It's nine o'clock at night on a school night."

"So?" he asked with wide-eyed innocence.

Tayde's phone rang for the fourth time.

"You'd better get that," he said helpfully, nodding at the phone in her hand.

With one last grunt, Tayde swiped her finger to answer the phone and said brightly, "Hi, Mom!"

"Good girl," Knox whispered before breezing out the door and shutting it firmly behind him.

"I tried to call earlier, but you didn't answer," her mom said, her tone slightly irritated. "Don't you get off work at five o'clock?"

Tayde sighed, trying to prepare herself for the unavoidable conversation. Vickie Wright's three children were of utmost importance in Vickie's life, and now that they were all adults, keeping up with every detail of their lives was her favorite hobby.

"I had our church small group barbecue tonight, remember?" Tayde said easily. "We decided to do it on the fifth so everyone could spend July fourth with families first."

"Oh, I didn't realize that was today," Vickie admitted, sounding slightly appeased. "It went late for a weekday night."

And there was slight chiding once again. Tayde was almost thirty years old, and her mom still disapproved of her staying up late on a "school night."

"I left early," Tayde offered. "They were starting to set off fireworks, but I had to get home. I have an assignment for work I needed to get done."

"An assignment? Like a writing assignment, or just editing?"

Tayde cringed, wishing she hadn't said anything. The excitement and curiosity in Vickie's voice increased her anxiety several notches. "It's writing," she confessed.

"Oh, Tayde, really?" Vickie's breath came in audible, excited bursts, and Tayde worried she might hyperventilate. "They want you to write an article? Dave, they want Tayde to write an article. A real article! I knew this new job was a godsend!"

"No, Mom. It's not—" Tayde frantically tried to think of a way to hold her mom's feet on the ground. The only thing worse than disappointing her mom was disappointing her when her hopes and dreams had grown to the size of Everest. "It's not exactly what I imagined. They want me to write more of an advertisement or tabloid article—something that will get attention. It's not exactly investigative journalism like I'd hoped."

"Tabloid?" she echoed incredulously. "Tayde, you can't write lies! I hope you told them no! You weren't hired to be paparazzi!"

Tayde opened her mouth and shut it, unsure of what had just happened and how to respond. She'd jumped from the frying pan into the fire. Finally, she leaned her head back against the couch and sighed, closing her eyes wearily. "No, Mom. Not that kind of tabloid. Nothing to do with celebrities. They just want me to write something that provides a headline someone might want to click on social media. I don't have to lie. It's just not serious writing. It's like the potato chips of the writing world."

"Oh, well, that's still not what you were hired for," she said haughtily. "Did you tell them that? You're the *main course*, not potato chips."

Tayde could picture her mom's hands on her hips as she readied to explain word-for-word what Tayde should tell her boss.

How did she explain to her mom that she really was at the potato chip level? A horrifying image popped into her head of her mom showing up at work to plead Tayde's case herself.

"It's a good opportunity, Mom," Tayde assured. She needed

to douse the fire, even if it meant not sharing her full feelings on the subject. "I have no writing experience, so maybe this will give me what I need to work myself up to the main course. At least I can use it on my resume to try to get a job somewhere else."

"But, Tayde, you are so much better than that," Vickie insisted. "They should see that. It's not fair that they promised you one thing and went back on their word."

Her mom would forever be Tayde's champion and believe in her to the exclusion of all reality. She knew she wasn't perfect and needed to work hard to improve, but she also knew there would be no convincing her mom that she wasn't already the best and simply a victim of others' incompetence.

Tayde studied the light overhead, noting it was dusty and needed cleaning. "They didn't promise me anything, Mom," she tried to explain. "I was hired as a writer for a magazine, but they didn't say what type of writer or what direction the magazine was going."

"Then they were deceitful for not giving you all the information," Vickie shot back adamantly.

Stifling a groan, Tayde slowly leaned over until her head met the couch. She just wanted the conversation to be over. She loved her mom, and she loved that she was fiercely loyal. But she wasn't always rational. There was no gray in Vickie's world, and there would be no changing her perception.

With a deep breath, she sat back up. If she could just convince her that she was fine, even if she wasn't. "It's okay, Mom," she kept her tone calm and upbeat. "It's a great opportunity. It's not what I wanted, but I can work my way up."

"Of course, you can," Vickie purred supportively. "I know you're disappointed, Tayde, but I'm not worried about you. You bounce. You'll be just fine. I worry more about your brother and sister." Her voice changed, worry threading it thickly. "All I can do is pray for them. All of you are adults and don't need to listen to your mom anymore."

And they'd moved to another familiar avenue. It was true that Vickie worried about Tayde the least. If something really bad happened to her, Vickie would tell her what to do, but that was usually the extent of her "help." She provided much more comfort and support to Tayde's siblings. Ever since she was a kid, Tayde was the one who carried the most responsibility and was the most independent. If Tayde and her sister fell down, Vickie would comfort Averie and send Tayde on her way, knowing she'd be okay because she "bounced."

But sometimes Tayde didn't feel like bouncing.

Tired of staring up at the dirty light, Tayde reached over and flipped the switch, eliminating the extra stimuli of light and letting the room exhale into darkness.

Tayde wanted to leave her mom's comment hanging and hope they could end the conversation, but she sat in the dark and took the bait. "Knox is fine, Mom. And last time I talked to Averie, she was doing fine too. She's waiting tables and thinking about taking a couple of college classes."

Vickie snorted. "Averie is still talking about going to Hollywood. She hasn't signed up for classes yet, and she doesn't like her new boss. She found a friend who lives in the L.A. area, and she's talking about moving down there and trying to get her big break. I just can't imagine sweet Averie in that horrible place. I won't sleep at all."

"It might be good for her, Mom," Tayde tried, even though she knew it was pointless. "She's always wondered about it. Her dream has always been acting. Maybe she'd either make it or get it out of her system."

"I can't believe you said that, Tayde!" Vickie gasped, offended.

"You want your little sister in that evil place?"

No. I want this conversation over.

She knew she wouldn't win. There was nothing she could say. Either she agreed with everything her mom said, which would feed into her worry and make it worse, or she disagreed and risked making her mom hurt and angry.

Feeling her stress level elevate, even with the room in blackness, Tayde turned and lifted her feet to stretch out along the length of the couch.

"Knox is fine," Tayde wearily attempted a redirect, trying to retreat and change the subject off Averie. "I just saw him. He's got a good job and looked well-fed and relatively clean. He didn't even have his shirt on backward when he went out the door. I checked."

"Tayde Wright, you know he is not fine," Vickie chastised, not appreciating Tayde's humor. "And it's not okay to joke about your brother when he needs our prayers."

"Okay, what am I missing?" Tayde asked, confused. "What do I need to pray for him about?"

"His women!" Vickie's incredulous voice almost sounded like a shriek. "He went on another late-night date, probably with a random girl he just met. He's not been the same since Britany. I just wish those two could have worked it out."

"She cheated on him, Mom." Tayde put her hand to her temple, trying to rub away the pain. This information was nothing new. Their conversation was an exact rerun. "They got divorced because she cheated on him."

"I don't believe it," Vickie's voice was tight and crisp. "Britany was such a nice girl. I think it all was a big misunderstanding. If they just talked…"

The pain in her temple wasn't going away. She moved her hand to her neck, trying to loosen the tension there. "It's been a year, Mom. I'm not going to pray they get back together. I know you always liked Britany, but I never did. She was fake. She was so nice to you, and when your back was turned, she was mean. She treated Knox terribly. But he's doing well now. He likes the school where he's teaching. Yes, he dates a lot, but none of it is serious. He's still very hurt, but he's not being stupid."

Knox owed her. Really owed her. He'd thrown her to the wolves, and now she was defending him.

"I just worry about him so," Vickie said, choking up with unshed tears. "No good Christian girl will marry a man who is divorced!"

"Just keep praying for him, Mom," Tayde said gently, finally resorting to the only argument her mother would ever accept. "That's all you can do."

"Oh, I do," Vickie sniffed. "I really do."

Tayde caught a slight glimmer at the end of the tunnel. "And you can pray for me about this assignment. I really need to go, Mom. I'm supposed to have the column done tomorrow, and I haven't started yet." She wasn't simply asking for prayers as a way to end the conversation. She did appreciate her prayers and felt a little frustrated with herself that she hadn't requested them sooner.

"You haven't started yet?" Vickie gasped. "Oh, Tayde! That's not like you! You don't usually wait until the last minute!"

Gah! Now she'd landed herself in more disappointment and chastising.

Tayde thought about telling her that she'd just gotten the assignment at five o'clock today. Then she'd gone to her church group barbecue, and now she was talking to her. So exactly when was she supposed to get it done?

But instead, she simply said, "I'll get it done in time. I'll talk to you later, Mom."

"Ok, chickadee," Vickie said lovingly. "You go write some beautiful words and show them how good you are. Love you, honey."

"Love you too, Mom. Bye."

Tayde ended the call with a huge sigh of relief. She tossed the phone lightly to the floor beside the couch and didn't even bother lifting her head for several minutes.

She needed to pull out her laptop and get to work, but she didn't know if she could manage any "beautiful words" tonight. Eventually, she dragged herself off the couch and carried her laptop bag into her bedroom, away from the lovely darkness.

She reluctantly flipped on the light. Hoping she could tackle it after she cleaned up, she showered and brushed her teeth. Unlike Knox, Tayde was not a night owl. She liked to be in bed about the time Knox liked to head out for a few hours of nightlife. From previous experience, she knew she wouldn't even hear him when he arrived home at around two o'clock in the morning. He'd be awake again at six o'clock, and she'd see him briefly before she headed off to the magazine, and he left for his job as a science teacher at a local junior high school.

Even with the light on, the call of her bed proved too strong, and she climbed under the covers. She placed multiple pillows at her back and tried to talk herself into any shred of determination to write a bunch of words under the stupid *Wrongs made Wright* title.

Determined, she reached down, pulled out her laptop, and opened it to retrieve the email from Sheryl. But an overwhelming wave of exhaustion and sadness overcame her.

She just couldn't do it tonight. She would look over the reader letter Sheryl wanted her to respond to, but that's it. She'd start thinking about it as she went to sleep. Then she'd be ready to write it tomorrow. She had time. She could write, edit, and have it ready by the end of tomorrow's workday.

She was too tired, and, given her stress level and the conversation with her mom, she knew the nightmares might visit again tonight. They weren't coming as often. After more than a dozen years, you'd think they'd leave her alone entirely. But if she were overly stressed, especially if some of that stress came from her parents, the nightmares would come to visit again. Of course, her mom didn't know she had nightmares at all. Tayde would never tell her. She'd never told anyone.

Tayde pulled up the email, and the attached letter filled the screen.

The dreams were stupid. She was fine. After all, she bounced.

To Whom it May Concern,

My husband and I witnessed something shocking and disrespectful this Fourth of July. This letter is to draw attention to the incident so that parents will teach their kids to be better humans and Americans.

Like many in our community, we enjoy the local Fourth of July fireworks show. Our community works hard to create such an amazing and patriotic display. As you know, the cemetery's position on the city's "bench area" is a great place to view the fireworks.

We got to the cemetery early to get good seats on the edge of the bluff. While we were waiting for dark, we witnessed a bunch of kids playing a game of baseball right over the graves. They were literally jumping over headstones and stepping on graves, and they ran, threw, and hit the ball that flew everywhere. I've never seen something so disrespectful. The young people were old enough to know better. And their parents were right there watching them!

On a holiday where we should be showing respect for our country and our history, this family was partying amongst the dead.

I didn't want to create a scene by confronting the family, but I hope they realize how disrespectful and unpatriotic such behavior is. Both the kids and their parents should be ashamed of themselves. Not only did they offend the dead with their blatant disrespect. They also ruined the holiday for those unfortunate enough to witness it. Shame on you!

Sincerely,
A Concerned Citizen

Dear Gravely Upset American,

A baseball game in a cemetery? Did they use headstones for the bases?

Our American society has reached a low point if our citizens throw Fourth of July parties on the graves of those who have come before us. How upsetting to witness something so appalling! I suggest you write to the city council and see about getting security for the cemetery next Fourth of July. If that is not an option, the cemetery may need to be closed for viewing if such disrespect continues. It is not acceptable behavior. There are plenty of other places to play baseball and party. A cemetery is not one of them.

It's concerning that kids would engage in such behavior. It's even more concerning that the parents didn't control their children and *teach them what respect looks like.*

But there is still hope. There are still a few who see the wrong and work to make it right, or in my case, Wright. With those of us shedding light on such situations, maybe there will come a day when we can enjoy a Fourth of July celebration at the cemetery with an attitude of respect, in remembrance of both those who fought for the freedom we enjoy and those who enjoyed the freedom before us.

May you continue to advocate for patriotism and respect for those who can no longer speak for themselves.

Sincerely
T. Wright

Chapter Three

Jarod

Jarod stepped out of the truck and stood for a moment, taking deep breaths as he tried to steel himself for the hour that lay ahead. His gaze drifted irresistibly in her direction. Even after all this time, he couldn't bear to look and yet couldn't bear not to look.

A wave of grief shuddered through him, and he leaned against the truck, letting it hold his weight for the briefest of seconds.

"We don't have to do this, Jarod."

The quiet voice came at his elbow, but it didn't startle him. He hadn't wanted the kids to see his turmoil, but he should have known he couldn't hide it from Gavin. As his best friend since kindergarten, college roommate, best man at his wedding, and unofficial second father to his children, Gavin could pretty much read his mind. He probably knew Jarod better than Jarod knew himself.

"We can go somewhere else," Gavin offered. "There's still time to find parking closer to the fireworks launch site."

"No. I want to be here," Jarod insisted, but his voice sounded thin to his own ears. "It's our tradition."

"A tradition you just started last year," Gavin pointed out. "You can always make a new tradition."

Jarod kept his eyes averted, not wanting Gavin to see what this was costing him. He wanted to do this. He wanted to be strong.

Hoping to gain control of his emotions, he focused on the sound of the kids hopping out of the truck and chatting on the other side. "No, I want her to be a part of it. I want the kids to feel she's with us, even in the fun things."

"But if it's too painful, Jarod, it's okay to do something else."

He heard the compassion in his friend's tone. Gavin had been there through everything and was waiting to hold him up if he fell. But Jarod wanted to stand. He needed to stand.

"I'm fine," he assured, successfully masking his emotions from his tone. "They shouldn't always feel sad when they think of their mom. This is a way of including her in a happy moment. It's like she's watching the fireworks with us."

Gavin nodded his acceptance, obviously knowing when to let something go. "Let's get the chairs set up. It's an hour before the show starts, but we need to reserve our spot."

Jarod walked around to the back of his truck and pulled open the tailgate. He could hear scuffling and grunting on the other side and knew without looking that his three sons were engaged in roughhousing that would put WWE stars to shame.

Jarod grabbed a foam baseball that had been rolling around

the truck's bed and stepped to the side. "Hey boys, go play baseball," he hollered, lobbing the ball in their direction.

His oldest son, Cody, caught it.

"We need a bat," the twelve-year-old insisted.

"See if you can find something that will work," Jarod replied, returning to continue his search for the chairs in the truck's bed.

He heard the scuffling as the three boys scampered back into the truck to search. Jarod hoped the search would keep them busy for a few minutes, but he was disappointed when he heard the sound of success less than thirty seconds later.

"Found it!" a cheerful voice called.

Jarod looked over to see his youngest son jump out of the truck wielding a large stick. With his brothers trailing in his wake, he jogged toward the open area beyond the rows of graves.

"Is that a tree branch?" Gavin asked, his tone slightly appalled but with a fair amount of admiration mixed in. "Where did they find that?"

Jarod shrugged. "A good stick, aka a baseball bat, is the holy grail of their existence. They picked it up somewhere. It's probably one of the less scary 'treasures' they've shoved into the truck's back seat."

"Nothing better than a good stick," Gavin agreed readily.

Jarod scanned the area. Thankfully, they were parked behind the occupied part of the cemetery. Beyond the neat, manicured rows of graves, a large, undeveloped area spanned the distance to the fence line that marked the edge of the property. They had parked in this large dirt area, and the boys were spreading out to mark their field.

Turning to his sons, Jarod called, "Hey, guys, stay in this open dirt area. Don't go over by the headstones. The grass is off-limits for you and the ball. Got it?"

Their focus remained on positioning large rocks to mark the bases.

"Come on, guys!" Jarod called impatiently. "Your upcoming game will be canceled unless I get confirmation that you have heard and will acquiesce to my expectations."

"Do they understand that foreign language?" Gavin muttered.

Cody immediately called back, "We have assimilated the intel and will comply with the prime directive! Stay off the grass, we will!"

"You guys are weird," Gavin concluded.

"You should know," Jarod quipped back. "I hope we're weird. Normal is no fun." He set one last lawn chair on the ground beside him and counted for the tenth time. "I'm short a chair. I must not have grabbed them all."

"I've got an extra in my truck," Gavin offered. "I'll grab it."

"Are you sure?" Jarod asked uncertainly. "Isn't Kendra coming to join us? I was surprised she didn't come with you to the barbecue. You know she was welcome."

They'd celebrated the holiday earlier with burgers at Jarod's house. His boys loved Gavin, and the holiday was made extra special that he'd come. Jarod had appreciated the help getting dinner ready while wrangling three wild boys. It had surprised him that Gavin's girlfriend hadn't come, but he hadn't yet had the chance to ask Gavin about it.

"Nah," Gavin said, his mouth scrunching into a half-scowl. "I mean, she would have. She was planning on it. But then we broke up this morning. So that ended that."

Jarod shot him a look that said he was surprised but not surprised. "Seriously, Gavin? I thought things were going well. You've been together a couple of months, which is a long relationship for you."

Jarod followed Gavin to his truck, where they retrieved his extra chair.

"Just wasn't feeling it," Gavin finally replied simply.

Jarod felt his mouth drop open. "Dude, she was gorgeous. How could you not feel it?"

Gavin shrugged. "It was superficial. We had a good time together, but we never had any meaningful, in-depth conversations. It was all fluff and no substance."

With their arms loaded with chairs, they walked over to the bluff. Finding an open spot, they set their chairs up, joining the long line of other spectators already reserving front-row seating. Jarod swung his chair around backward to face the cemetery instead of the bluff. He sat down, satisfied that he had prime viewing of his kids and their game. Gavin followed suit and sat in the chair beside him.

"Did you try?" Jarod asked pointedly. Gavin was a serial dater. He wasn't sure what his best friend's issue was. It wasn't commitment. It wasn't that he enjoyed partying. He was a serious, high-character Christian guy. But Gavin managed to find something wrong with every single girl he ever dated. Like Goldilocks' search for perfect, Gavin had never found a girl who was "just right."

A sigh escaped Gavin's lips. "I know what you're getting at, Jarod. Trust me, it's my problem, not hers, and I know it. I thought about taking the relationship to a deeper level. I considered asking her some thought-provoking questions, but it felt like too much work. It sounds terrible, but I didn't care enough to want to know what she thought about deeper issues. I want someone I can talk to for what feels like five minutes, look at the clock, and realize we've talked for hours. I want to care what she thinks and how she thinks. I want to respect and value her opinion more than anyone else's but God's."

"Gavin, I hate to tell you this, but relationships are work." Was that Gavin's problem? Was he looking for an ideal that didn't exist? Gavin had certainly seen enough of his relationship with Tory to know good marriages weren't perfect.

"I get that," Gavin nodded. "I just didn't want to put the work into this one."

Realizing Gavin didn't have any solid explanations for the breakup, Jarod gave up the interrogation. "That's too bad. I liked Kendra."

Gavin saw his youngest son smack a solid hit over his brother's head and take off running. The other players scrambled to get the ball while Max rounded the bases and headed for home. The play ended with a throw to home and Max sliding into the patch of weeds that doubled as home plate. Max immediately jumped up, and the fight was on as Cody and Trey argued over whether or not Max was safe.

"Don't get me wrong; Kendra is great," Gavin said. "She's just not the one for me." Gavin's eyes lit up. "In fact, maybe you should ask her out."

Jarod choked on his own saliva. It took him several seconds to recover as he seriously considered laughing Gavin's suggestion off. He'd done that plenty of times when Gavin had brought up the dating subject before. But this time, he didn't. He paused, thinking about it for the first time since Tory passed. Well, maybe he wasn't thinking about it. He was just thinking about thinking about it.

"Don't think I'm ready for that, Gavin," he admitted slowly as he watched the boys continue to argue. "You can't find your one, but I already had mine. She made the work worth it. Loving her was easy. Putting the work in to be worthy of her was hard."

Keeping his eyes on the scene before him, he realized his

sons wouldn't solve the disagreement independently. Seeing that they were about two seconds from coming to blows, Jarod raised his voice and shouted, "He was safe!"

"You can't call it from there!" Cody protested indignantly.

"I can because I'm the dad!" Jarod called back.

Cody grumbled his way back to the circle in the dirt designated as the pitching mound, and the game finally resumed.

"It's been two years, Jarod," Gavin brought up gently. "Tory wanted you to find someone else."

Jarod felt anger immediately flare, not at Gavin but at the world in general. He hated cliches, and he'd heard them all. Gavin wasn't one to fling empty platitudes around, but this was one he'd heard before and hated.

"That's what they always say," Jarod gritted out. "But Tory isn't here to give me the message herself. It's just a lot. The thought of bringing someone new around the kids terrifies me. Maybe after they're grown. But I don't know that Tory would want me to find someone right now." He held out his hand, indicating the game in front of them. "The boys would get in a brawl, and any woman in her right mind would turn and run!"

"Jarod, Max is eight. That'll be a long time if you're waiting for his eighteenth birthday. It's not a cliché. Not when I say it. Tory wanted you to remarry, and she didn't put parameters on when you could. In fact, she was kinda keeping an eye out for you before she died."

Jarod felt his stomach turn. "Gavin, stop. You can't know any of that. It's all conjecture. You don't know what she was thinking and feeling."

"I *do* know," Gavin insisted. Then he paused as if overcome with his own wave of grief. He looked from the game to the setting sun in the west.

When he spoke again, his words were quiet. "I know because she told me." He didn't look at Jarod, and each syllable was heavy with tightly controlled emotion. "Remember that day she found out she was terminal? The boys had baseball practice, and you had to coach. You called me, and I showed up at the field after work. Tory was sitting under a tree all alone, watching you and the boys play. I sat on the grass beside her and just listened. While we watched baseball, Tory unloaded every thought and feeling crowding her heart and mind, and I listened. You sometimes wonder what you would think and feel if you found out you only have a few months to live. I don't wonder anymore. I know."

Jarod tried to focus on the game, watching the stick do its duty admirably as each kid took a turn sending the foam ball flying. But he couldn't quite distract himself enough from his friend's unexpected confession. His throat thickened, and he responded huskily, "I didn't know that. You never told me."

"No, I didn't," Gavin said without a hint of regret. "You had enough grief. You didn't need to hear the details of hers." He paused, taking a deep breath before continuing. She was worried about you, Jarod." She said you were too good of a husband to be alone. She wanted you to find someone else to love and be a husband to."

Jarod didn't doubt the truth of Gavin's words, but they were hard to hear. He desperately wished Gavin would stop and leave him to watch the dirt fly beneath the feet of the base runners.

Gavin's voice changed, and he laughed lightly, though it didn't quite chase away the flavor of grief. "She actually said she needed to find you a new wife before she died."

Jarod felt a chuckle bubble up in response. "That sounds like her. She preferred to plan every detail of every detail."

"Yes, she did," Gavin said simply.

Jarod thought about asking Gavin about more of that conversation with Tory. What else had she said? But then he decided he didn't want to know. Gavin was right. Jarod still wasn't ready to hear about her grief. She'd passed two years ago, and his grief still overwhelmed him. Tory had been so strong. She'd shielded him and the kids from her turmoil and focused on them. He felt glad Gavin had been there in the moment she'd needed him. Despite the unimaginable pain she'd felt as cancer destroyed her body, she'd smiled until the day she graduated to heaven.

He heard a beep and automatically picked up his phone to see the notification of an incoming text.

"That's Kendra's number," Gavin said casually. "Just in case you want to text her sometime."

Jarod didn't respond.

"And, yes, she'd go out with you," Gavin assured, successfully reading Jarod's thoughts. "Let me know if you'll let me spend some time with my favorite boys one evening so you can go out."

"Thanks, Gavin. But keeping up with your girlfriend castoffs will take a lot of work." Infusing his words with a little humor brought a sense of relief. He was ready to steer the conversation to safer waters. "I'm not in your league."

Gavin grinned. "No worries, Jarod. I'll send a steady supply headed your way."

"That's what I'm afraid of," he replied dryly.

Jarod turned back to his kids, noting that the game now included numerous other kids playing, running around imaginary bases, and squealing with glee.

"They're kinda loud," he observed, nervously glancing down the line of lawn chairs parked on the bluff. "Do you think

I need to tell them to settle down?"

Many of the chairs held occupants waiting for the fireworks show to start. And many of the occupants looked like their childhood days were long past. They may not remember the joy of an impromptu baseball game played with a stick.

"No, they're fine," Gavin assured. "Let them play. They are following your prime directive and staying out of the grass and the graves. Besides, Tory would love this."

A soft smile lifted the corners of his mouth. "You're right. She would."

Tory had loved baseball. It's one of the things they'd had in common. They'd vacationed to see major league baseball games, and it had thrilled her when her own boys were old enough to start playing the game. The St. Louis Cardinals had been her team, and the boys' favorite apparel was still Cardinals gear. Jarod didn't know if it was more because they loved the Cardinals or because they loved their mom. They practically wouldn't wear anything but Cardinals red.

Jarod's gaze drifted over to her grave. He could see the stone and the flowers beside it. Somehow, he still felt the shock. Part of him couldn't believe she lay over there in a box in the ground. He knew she wasn't *really* there. He reminded himself frequently that she was in Heaven, out of pain and experiencing happiness and peace he could only imagine. But he still felt closer to her here by the tangible piece of who she'd been on earth. He brought the boys here often to "visit their mom." They always brought flowers, and he taught them to tend after her grave.

Now, as he watched his boys, he felt the discrepancy between their youthful joy and play contrasted with the grief of the graves and death that lay beyond their play. And he felt it was right somehow. Maybe a cemetery shouldn't be such a sad place. Maybe the dead would approve of the life happening beside them.

It was almost as if Jarod could feel Tory's presence and feel her pleasure at seeing her boys play baseball on the Fourth of July. It's what she would have wanted in life, and Jarod still desperately wanted to give it to her, even in death.

The sun's last tendrils of light began to fade, and Jarod didn't know how the kids were still managing to see their foam baseball.

"Come on, boys! Time for fireworks!" Jarod called, reluctantly ending the epic game.

Though there were a few groans of disappointment, all three boys obeyed, gathered their ball and stick, and came trotting to the lawn chairs.

They settled in, and the boys eagerly started pointing out the random private fireworks around the valley below. The flashes of light vanished almost as soon as they pointed. Jarod loved the squeals of delight. A few minutes later, the sky was wrapping itself in velvety black when it suddenly burst with brilliant color at the start of the show.

Jarod felt a wave of peace steal over him as his view filled with a kaleidoscope and his ears caught the oohs and aahs whispered in children's voices.

He turned his head, casting one more quick look over his shoulder in her direction before turning back to the show. He felt her love and her joy. Somehow, he knew she was watching with them.

"Hey, Jarod, where are you?" Gavin's voice came breathless and urgent.

"I'm at home," he said warily. He didn't like Gavin's tone. "Why?"

"Are the kids there with you?" Jarod sounded like he'd been running.

Alarm shot through Jarod. He immediately walked over to the window above the kitchen sink and looked out, counting the three figures running around the yard. "Yeah. They're outside playing baseball. I'm getting ready to make dinner. Why?"

"I just got off work. I'm bringing pizza over. I'll be there in fifteen minutes. And, Jarod? Don't look at social media."

"Um... why?"

But Gavin was gone.

Jarod wasn't much on social media. He had an account, but he rarely checked it. And he wasn't one to go against his best friend's recommendation. But he couldn't imagine why Gavin would say such a thing. No scenario he imagined could account for Gavin's weird behavior. Had something awful happened in the world?

Of course, that made him curious.

So, of course, he opened the app on his phone.

It didn't take long. Multiple friends had already shared the article, and he saw several social media ads before he drummed up the courage to click and read it. There were several versions of the headline, most of which sparked curiosity.

A Grave New Sports Venue

Fourth of July Strikeout

He finally naively clicked on the one with the most ridiculous headlines of them all: *First Base died in 1972.*

As soon as he read the letter's first line, he knew. He read through the whole thing, anger boiling in him. But the words of T. Wright's responding letter drew tears.

He was reading the entire thing a third time when he heard Gavin's voice behind him.

"No, Jarod!" Gavin moaned. "I told you not to look!"

He felt the phone slip through his hand as Gavin removed it, turned off the screen, and set it on the counter.

Jarod looked up at Gavin. The empathy in his friend's eyes was his undoing. The numb shock gave way. He'd spent the last two years trying to keep his emotions in check. Gavin had been there to catch his tears right after Tory had passed, and Jarod had managed to keep a lid on them ever since. He didn't want the kids to feel his grief in addition to their own. But they were outside, Gavin was here, and the letters…

The wall came down. Great, heaving sobs shook his shoulders, and he buried his head in his hands. He'd tried so hard to do the right thing. To grieve the right way. To care for three motherless children.

And the words he'd just read devastated him. It was like they took his grief and used it to slap him in the face.

He desperately wished the pain would stop.

Heaving in a ragged breath, he lifted his head and looked at Gavin, his words coming brokenly. "I was trying to… I didn't mean to…" But he couldn't get out a single coherent thought.

Gavin bent down so he faced him at eye level. It was like he was trying to absorb some of Jarod's grief and replace it with strength. He radiated compassion and acceptance, but all he said was a murmured, "I know… I know…"

And at that moment, that's exactly what Jarod needed.

Chapter Four

Tayde wasn't aware of when the murmurs started. With her focus on her computer screen and her head bowed in her cubicle, she sorted through hundreds of reader letters, separating them into piles for no and maybe. She had no idea the magazine received this much mail in one week. Even more daunting was the fact she needed to pick one letter to respond to. It was like sorting through a dumpster hoping to find a diamond.

Someone passed behind her, the movement disrupting her focus. She blinked and looked around as if suddenly waking to the world around her. Slowly, she realized the room was silent, void of the usual steady clicks of fingers on keyboards. Like the ever-present chirping of crickets, you don't notice the sound until it's absent.

She lifted herself off her chair slightly, peering over the cubicle partitions. Numerous gazes met her own but immediately dashed away at the contact.

What was going on? Was everyone staring at her?

A notification sounded on her computer, signaling the arrival of an email.

Tayde plopped back down in her seat and brought up her inbox.

A message from Sheryl popped on the screen.

```
My office. Now.
```

The words sent a bucket of ice water over Tayde. What was going on? She desperately wanted to take a quick scroll online or check through the rest of her messages, but she didn't dare to take the time.

She stood, smoothed her skirt, and scurried toward Sheryl's office. She felt the eyes of everyone in the room follow her. There was no doubt. Something was wrong.

She cast a frantic glance at Frankie's cubicle. Frankie was the tech wizard at the magazine and Tayde's friend in her off-hours. They'd met at church, and Frankie was the one who'd told Tayde about the job opening for a writer at the magazine.

But Tayde could only glimpse the top of her friend's head. Frankie was apparently the only person in the room with her head down working. Tayde had no hope of getting her attention to ask what was happening.

Tayde frantically scanned her memory, wondering what she'd done. Her first *Wrongs Made Wright* column had come out yesterday. She was too busy and nervous to babysit it every minute of the day, but it looked like it had done well so far, garnering numerous shares and positive comments.

Had something happened that she didn't know about?

Tayde knocked briefly on the gray door before opening it.

She mentally prepared to announce herself and waited patiently while Sheryl ignored her in favor of her computer screen.

But Sheryl wasn't sitting in front of her computer. She was standing in front of her desk, pacing back and forth. A quick glance revealed the office to look the same as at Tayde's last visit, with one exception. A cat sat in the center of Sheryl's desk.

"Have you seen it?" Sheryl immediately demanded.

"Seen what?" Tayde asked. Desperately, she tried to read the emotion behind Sheryl's flashing eyes. Was it excitement or anger? A huge boulder lodged in Tayde's throat. Was she about to get fired?

Sheryl waved her hands impatiently. "The letter. The comment. The response to your column."

Tayde slowly shook her head. She had no idea what Sheryl was talking about.

"What have you been doing—hiding under a rock?" Sheryl hissed impatiently. She hurried back behind her desk and bent over to bring something up on her computer. As she did, the cat arched its back toward her, rubbing its shiny black fur against the sleeve of Sheryl's designer suit. Though Tayde had never had a boss who kept a pet in her office, the cat seemed like a nice one. With his tuxedo coloring, he looked rather important and regal using Sheryl's desk as his throne.

Finding what she wanted, Sheryl jerked the computer screen to angle in Tayde's direction. "There! Read that!"

Tayde crept closer, not sure what to expect.

The first words caught her attention. It was a letter to her. With mounting dread, she began reading.

Dear Ms. Wright,

I know a family who, like your Gravely Concerned American, witnessed the incident that was described in your column. They were at the cemetery on the evening of the Fourth of July. Their names are Jarod and Tory Paulsen, and they were there enjoying the holiday as a family. Jarod Paulsen is a construction manager and dad to three boys. You might find it more difficult to find information about Tory. The best place to look is her obituary from two years ago.

This is not the Paulsens' first visit to the cemetery as a family. Their first visit was for Tory's funeral. Everyone wore red because Tory was the biggest baseball fan ever, and her team was the St. Louis Cardinals. At the close of the service, she was laid to rest as everyone sang, "Take Me Out to the Ballgame."

Just like last Fourth of July, Jarod brought his three boys to the cemetery to watch the fireworks with their mom. While waiting for the festivities, they played baseball with a foam ball and a stick in the open area behind the graves. They have been taught to respect and tend to their mother's grave, and they were careful to follow their dad's instructions by keeping their play out of the cemetery area.

So, they played a game of baseball for their mom to "watch." To a casual passerby, the story behind the game was not obvious, but Jarod would have been happy to answer any questions or talk about his wife if anyone were to have asked. Next time, I pray you and your readers will take the time to learn the backstory before assuming the worst.

Jarod would like to offer an apology to anyone they unknowingly offended, recognizing that not everyone grieves the same way. Maybe our "Gravely Concerned American" was reacting based on his or her own personal story. The hurt Jarod has experienced due to assumptions is not something he wants to inflict on someone else.

I know everyone is different, but for the record, when I die, please play baseball in my graveyard. And hopefully, the good Lord will let me watch.

Can you hear the bells

"Is this true?" Tayde whispered, barely managing to get sound out of her tightly constricting throat.

"Yes," Sheryl answered firmly. "I read Tory Paulsen's obituary from two years ago."

Tayde moaned lightly and put her hands to her temples. She felt like she was going to pass out. Even the cat seemed to be glaring at her. She really needed to sit, but of course, the only chair in Sheryl's office was her own. She might just plop onto the desk, except she didn't think the cat would appreciate the company.

What had she done? She'd hurt and humiliated a grieving family and made the magazine look completely incompetent. "I had no idea!" she whispered hoarsely.

"I know!" Sheryl exclaimed. "You can't plan stuff like this."

Tayde's mind shifted to damage control. "Can we delete the comment? I can issue an apology to the Paulsens, but if we prevent more people from seeing it, it will be like it never happened. Or should we just delete the whole column?"

"Delete?" Sheryl asked as if she'd bitten into a rotten apple. "Why would I want to delete anything? Are you kidding? I gave that comment its own URL!"

Shocked, Tayde turned to Sheryl and really looked at her. Her face flushed, and her eyes sparkled. But maybe it wasn't with anger. Maybe it was excitement.

Hesitantly, Tayde asked, "Wait. Are you *happy* about this?"

Sheryl looked at her incredulously. "Why wouldn't I be? We can't buy this publicity! Both the column and Mr. Bells' response went viral! We've already started ads for it. Look at this one. *Anonymous Do-Gooder Puts Magazine Writer* in her place. Or this one: *Touché, Mr. Bells*. And this one, *A Graveyard Homerun*. We're working on more headlines. But these are already getting us lots of hits to the website!"

But none of those were flattering to her or the magazine. They didn't paint either one in a favorable light. And Sheryl was okay with that?

"So, you aren't mad?" Tayde asked, desperately trying to assess what was going on. Sheryl's reaction wasn't what she expected. And she couldn't figure out what she was supposed to feel about all of this.

"No, I'm thrilled!" Sheryl gushed. "I called you in here because I want to move up the date of your next column. I want it to go out on Monday."

Tayde shook her head, trying to catch up. "But shouldn't we apologize? I mean, it makes us look bad. It makes *me* look bad. I just roasted a grieving family in a column that went viral."

Sheryl shrugged. "No apology necessary. You didn't do anything wrong. He roasted you back."

Tayde disagreed. "No, he was nice about it. I wasn't. I would feel better if we made some kind of acknowledgment."

Sheryl turned the computer screen away from Tayde. "Sorry. You don't get to feel better. You did your job. Feel good about that. You wrote a column that got clicks and publicity for our website. You launched us even better than I anticipated. Now I want you to do it again."

"Do it again?" Tayde was appalled. "You want me to find

someone else to offend?"

"Absolutely."

Tayde's look of horror must have clipped Sheryl's wings slightly. She sighed and continued in a tone that said she was trying to pacify her. "Look, you don't have to offend anyone. The magic of this column was that you elicited emotion. People cared. First, they were offended by Gravely Concerned American. Then they were shocked and grieved by Mr. Bells' letter. It made people *feel*. That's what you need to do again."

"Mr. Bells? Is that his name?" Tayde hadn't seen a name attached to the bottom of the letter. She reached out and turned the computer screen back, ready to look again. Who is he?"

Sheryl shrugged. "I have no idea. That's just what I called him because he said something about bells when he signed the letter. The account he posted from doesn't use his real name."

Tayde reached out and scrolled through the letter, searching for clues. "Maybe we could find out who he is, and I could contact him. I'd like to get the Paulsens' address and send a private apology. It doesn't have to be public."

"No," Sheryl said flatly, her tone allowing no hint of a counterargument. This time she turned the screen back and flipped it off. "Moving on."

"What if he responds again?" Tayde hadn't recovered from the first time. The thought of a second time was paralyzing.

Sheryl pressed her hands together in a praying gesture and looked up. "We should be so lucky. If only fortune shined on us a second time."

Alarm shot up inside Tayde. Sheryl wanted publicity at any cost, even if it hurt people and shredded Tayde's reputation in the process. "I don't know that I'm okay with being the court jester," Tayde said bravely. "I don't like the 'any news is good news' mentality."

Sheryl gave a longsuffering sigh. "You did a good job on the first column, Tayde. Much better than I would have anticipated, and I thought that before Mr. Bells commented and launched it viral. You don't have to sacrifice your integrity or purposely paint a train wreck with words for readers to ogle. Part of what made it so good was that it wasn't sensational. It was sincere. Gravely American was sincere. Your response was sincere. And Mr. Bells' response to that was sincere. Nothing was overly dramatized, purposely false, or grandiose. It was genuine. I need you to do that same thing again. We have an audience now. You'll undoubtedly get a lot more mail to choose from. Choose something tame. Something that's safe and won't risk a response from Mr. Bells. I don't care. Just be genuine."

Sheryl's words sounded almost nice. But underneath it all, Tayde recognized her motivation. She wanted Tayde to give a repeat performance and didn't really care about the costs or consequences. She was just telling Tayde what she wanted to hear to get the job done.

Tayde didn't have a choice if she wanted to keep her job. Idly, she reached out to pet the cat still watching her from the desk. The cat watched as her fingers neared the sleek fur on his neck. Then his mouth opened, and he hissed.

Tayde pulled her hand back, offended that the nice kitty wasn't nice at all!

Sheryl didn't seem to notice the interaction, and when Tayde didn't respond immediately, Sheryl offered, "I could pick another reader letter for you if that would help. I obviously did a good job with the last one!"

"No!" Tayde said hurriedly. "I can do it. I've already been sorting through them."

Sheryl walked behind her desk and reached her hand out in a long stroke to the cat's fur. A loud purr emanated as the cat's spine curled up in enjoyment.

"Then I'll expect your column by Sunday evening at the latest," she instructed. "I need it ready to go first thing Monday morning."

Tayde glared at the cat, mostly because she couldn't glare at Sheryl. Now Tayde knew what she'd be doing this weekend—writing and then agonizing, imagining a repeat performance from Mr. Bells.

She could only stomach doing it if she did it on her terms, not Sheryl's. Tayde bit her lip before venturing, "I can do it, but I don't think that gives me enough time to research. I'd like to prevent another incident. If I can do a little investigation, I could write a—"

"No research! No investigation!" Sheryl's eyes flashed again, but she wasn't excited this time. "We aren't that type of magazine. Feel-good, mushy, dramatic—any of that is fine. But there is no need for research. Just get it done. Understand?"

Tayde knew when she'd pushed as far as she could go. The cat's narrowed green glare said he might be ready to attack at Sheryl's slightest encouragement. Seeing she was trapped, Tayde resigned herself to her fate and said, "You'll have it by Sunday."

Sheryl finally sat behind her desk and pulled the cat into her lap. He settled against her, the purr beginning immediately. Tayde knew she'd been dismissed.

She walked out of the office feeling like a horrible human being. She'd written something that hurt someone. She couldn't apologize. Now she had to do it again or lose her job. Had she just traded everything good about herself to keep a job?

Tayde walked back to her cubicle, trying to keep her emotions in. She wanted to go home, curl up on her bed, and cry. But she still had several hours of the workday left.

"You okay, Tayde?"

Tayde's stride paused at the fierce whisper. She turned to see Frankie leaning her head partway out of her cubicle. Tayde scanned the room, checking to ensure no eyes were on her before ducking inside the small space.

"She won't let me apologize," Tayde whispered. "She's just interested in the attention for the magazine. She wants me to write another column and doesn't care how it looks."

Frankie nodded. "I'm not surprised. What are you going to do?"

Tayde shrugged. "What can I do? The new column is supposed to come out Monday morning." She bit her lip, trying to keep it from trembling. "I just feel so terrible. Frankie, did you read the letter? That poor family! They were spending time with their mom, and she loved baseball. It didn't even sound like they were near the graves."

"Gravely American probably exaggerated because he or she was offended. Complaints are rarely completely accurate." Frankie said it all so factually like it wasn't upsetting at all.

"I have to apologize. Sheryl won't even try to identify Mr. Bells. Frankie, you're our tech guru. Do you think you can—"

"No way, Tayde," Frankie interrupted before Tayde could officially ask the question. "It's not worth both our jobs."

"But what if it happens again? What if I get it wrong again? Sheryl doesn't want research, but what if I hurt someone again? What if Mr. Bells responds again with another zinger and humiliates me again?"

Frankie's mouth turned up with humor. "That's a lot of 'again.' I don't think he humiliated you, Tayde. He could have, but he didn't. I thought he was kind of nice about it. You're the one in control here. You choose the letter. You write the response. Choose a touching topic no one will want to go near—kids, pets, something really heartwarming. Then write his pants off. Write a column so good he won't dare to respond."

Tayde giggled. "Write his pants off?"

Frankie smiled. "Figuratively, of course."

"He kind of wrote my pants off, didn't he?" she giggled again.

"Well, I wasn't going to say anything." Frankie tipped her head and looked away innocently. Then she turned back and speared Tayde with her fierce green eyes. "Sheryl stuck the pen in your hand. Use. It."

"Figurative, again. I use a computer, not a pen."

Frankie nodded agreeably. "Of course. The pen is in the pants, so to speak."

Tayde gasped and held her breath, trying to hold in peals of laughter. "You're bad for my health!" she choked out.

Frankie shook her head, "Not so. For your mental health, I'm amazing."

"Thanks, Frankie." Tayde sighed. "I'm off to find a pen and some pants."

"Better also include a good puppy dog letter to be right about," Frankie suggested.

Tayde ticked off her fingers as if counting off a list. "Pen, pants, puppy dog. Got it."

And prayer. A whole lot of prayer.

Tayde slipped out of the cubicle and headed to her own. She ignored the stares sent in her direction and focused on a quick prayer.

Lord, help me to write this column. Help me to not screw it up. And help Mr. Bells to stay silent.

Dear T. Wright,

I'm sixteen years old. I've never been to a dance. I've never even been on a date. I'm a good student, and I don't get in trouble. I have a few friends, but not many. I'm quiet and try to be nice to everyone. I've been working on being more social and making more friends. I want my high school memories to be more than studying with my head in books.

The last week of September is Homecoming at my school. I finally got the courage to ask a girl to the Homecoming dance. I didn't go for the most popular girl. I thought it would be safe to ask a girl who is smart, quiet, and nice. She's in a lot of my advanced classes, and we've gone to school together since the sixth grade. She's pretty too.

I was really nervous, but after one of our classes, I went up to her in the hall and asked if she'd go to the dance with me.

She replied, "Get away from me!" Then she hurried off. She didn't even look at me.

I don't think what she did was right. It's fine if she didn't want to go, but why couldn't she have been nice about it? Girls always say they want nice guys, but they don't really.

Can you explain to me why someone who acts nice would treat someone else like that? Is this how things are done? I just want girls to not be so mean to guys, even if they don't like them. I don't think I'll ever ask another girl out because now I know nice guys really do finish last.

Sincerely,
Not Going to the Homecoming Dance

Dear Nice Guy,

How awful for you! The way you were treated is not right. Unfortunately, it happens way too often. Yes, girls say they want nice guys, but a girl will trade nice for exciting and not even realize she's done it.

People need to be more aware of how they treat others. There is no excuse for how she treated you. There are many other ways she could have responded. Since education in this area is obviously lacking, here is a lesson in etiquette for today's generation. If someone asks you out:

Option 1: Say yes. A dance or a date is not a lifetime commitment. If he or she is a nice, safe person and at least worthy of friendship, say yes.

Option 2: Say no. "Thank you for asking, but... I'd rather just be friends. I already have plans. I don't like dances. Maybe next time."

Just about anything would be better than "Get away from me."

Thank you for sharing your experience. Though I cannot fix the wrong done to you, hopefully we can prevent that same wrong from happening to others.

If you are a parent of a teenage girl or a woman of any age, I hope you read Nice Guy's story and pay attention. We need to be better. If you truly want nice guys to finish first, you need to "get away" from issuing toxic cruelty to others and learn to be nice yourself.

Sincerely,
T. Wright

Chapter Five

Amelia

Amelia opened her locker and slid the textbooks onto the shelf. She reached into her backpack and grabbed the soft-sided lunchbox.

Lunchtime. The time of day she hated most. Nothing like being alone in a crowd of people. She always felt like such a reject. If she could, she'd go hide out alone in the girls' locker room like she usually did before school. But the idea of eating lunch in a locker room was kind of gross, and she didn't want to leave Vashti to sit alone.

She glanced at the magnetic mirror on her locker door. Sad, tired eyes looked back at her. She'd been up too late doing homework. With a sigh, she pushed her glasses up her nose and resigned to the realization that there was nothing she could do to change the appearance of the girl staring back.

She slammed the locker door and turned toward the lunchroom. The hallway opened into a wide atrium with round tables and chairs haphazardly crammed into the space. The room was crowded with students eating and visiting. Amelia hurried to her usual table at the edge of the room by a pillar, but she hesitated at the sight of a group of girls in the same area. Some were standing, and a few were sitting in chairs from the table, but they weren't using the table itself.

Should she go somewhere else? But this was where Vashti was supposed to meet her. Amelia guessed that her friend was finishing a test. Amelia didn't own a cell phone, so there was no way she could let Vashti know of a change of plans.

Amelia scanned the area, but there were no open tables. Cautiously, she approached the opposite side of the table. She slid a chair around so it angled away from the group of girls and sat down. She felt conspicuous, especially when she compared her thrift store sweater and jeans with their trendy outfits. But hopefully, they wouldn't even notice her.

She unzipped her lunchbox and pulled out a sandwich.

"You, like, always sit here," a voice said.

Amelia looked up to see one of the girls addressing her with a scowl.

"And you always have cold lunch," she continued. "Why?"

Amelia wasn't sure how to respond. Which statement did the why apply to—her location, her lunch, or both? Not wanting to speak with her mouth full, she carefully set her sandwich back on its wrapper and answered. "I'm waiting for a friend. I bring my lunch because I have allergies. I can't eat hot lunch, and I don't have a car to eat off campus."

"What are you allergic to?" another girl asked curiously.

Amelia recognized the girls. They were a year older than her and popular. This was the first time they'd ever noticed her existence. "Lots of things," she answered quietly. "Like peanuts."

"So, you're, like, allergic to this peanut butter cup?" the first girl asked, waving the candy bar around.

Yes. Deathly allergic. But all she did was nod.

"So, like, how much would it take to kill you?" she asked. "If I accidentally smeared a little on your sandwich and you ate it, would you die? Or would someone have to shove it down your throat?"

The twittering sound of the girls' giggles echoed in the room. Amelia didn't respond. She took her sandwich in her hand and angled her body more in the opposite direction.

But they weren't done.

"Are you going to Homecoming?" one of the girls asked her.

"Shhh. Leave her alone," another admonished. "Who would ask *her*?"

Trying to distract herself, Amelia finally took a bite of her sandwich. Then she wished she hadn't. It stuck in her throat as tears burned the back of her eyes.

She saw movement and looked up to see Vashti approaching. Amelia grabbed her lunch and made a beeline to meet her before she arrived.

"Let's go outside," she said quickly.

"We can't. It's raining," Vashti replied.

"We can't go over there," Amelia said, nodding back the way Vashti had come.

"Why not? A couple of those girls are in my art class. They're nice."

Amelia's throat constricted. It wouldn't do any good to explain what had happened. Vashti wouldn't believe her. No one would. Vashti would probably say she'd read too much into it.

"You can go if you want," Amelia offered. "I'm done eating." She had only choked down one bite but had no appetite to take another.

"Sheesh, Amelia. You're so anti-social. It's okay to be friendly." Vashti looked from Amelia back to the girls, clearly torn. However, it was obvious where she wanted to be.

"You go ahead, Vashti. I've got to get my books out of my locker for my next class.

Amelia didn't wait for a response but hurried back to her locker. She stowed her full lunchbox back inside and loaded her backpack with books. Unfortunately, she still had more time to kill, so she snuck away to the girls' locker room.

The back of the room connected to the ladies' restroom used during sporting events. Since its entrance was on the opposite side of the gym, it wasn't used during the school day. Amelia crept through the door and shut it behind her. She set her backpack on a corner bench across from the line of toilets. Then she sat beside it. No one would bother her here. She drew her knees up onto the bench and wrapped her arms around them. Then she laid her head on her knees and tried to fight back the tears.

She couldn't cry now. If she did, her eyes would be red and ugly when the bell rang for class in seven minutes. And her glasses would make her red eyes look even bigger and uglier. She took deep breaths in and out, listening to the silence as she tried to calm herself down.

It was okay. She was okay. Vashti was a good friend. She just hadn't known what had happened. If she'd been there, Vashti would have told the girls off. But since she hadn't seen and heard their behavior herself, any report from Amelia would have been attributed to Amelia's misinterpretation of events.

The bell finally rang, though it sounded muted from this

side of the school. Amelia gathered her backpack, slipped back through the locker room, and made her way to English class. Keeping her head down to avoid making eye contact, she made it up the stairs and started down the hall.

"Hey, Amelia!"

Amelia looked up to see Damien Dorsey grinning at her. Then, slowly, Damien licked his lips and pumped his eyebrows suggestively. The boys with him burst into peals of laughter.

Amelia ducked her head and rushed away, her face burning in humiliation, swerving around backpacks and other students like a wild car in a racing video game.

Oomph!

"Watch where you're going!"

"Oh, sorry!" Amelia apologized. Seeing the room number over the door overhead, she sprinted to the classroom and entered the door at a walk, acting as if nothing were wrong. She found her usual desk and took out her notebook, ready for class to begin.

Damien and his cronies arrived a minute later and took their seats. They said nothing, and Amelia didn't acknowledge their presence.

Thankfully, the rest of the class passed quickly, and Amelia could focus on her work and block everything else out. When the bell rang to end the class, Amelia waited until everyone cleared out before exiting. Making her way to her last class of the day, she passed by a large group of students, including Damien Dorsey, clustered around the stairwell.

Amelia tucked her head down and tried to hurry past.

"Hey, what about her?" a voice said loudly. "Why don't you ask *her*?"

Amelia couldn't help but look. Sure enough, the boys were pointing directly at her. The way the question was phrased was obviously not a compliment, and roars of laughter echoed through the building as soon as it was voiced.

She was the butt of the joke, and she knew it.

It hurt. Oh, it hurt. But there was no shock. The lip-licking and comments were almost daily occurrences, especially from that group of boys. But Amelia never breathed a word about it to anyone. She just endured. The boys were well-liked by both students and teachers. It would do no good to complain. No one would believe her. Besides, what was there to complain about? Comments and teasing were normal parts of school, right? It was all normal. It was just Amelia who was *abnormal*.

She made it to her history class. To her relief, they watched a video. With the classroom lights lowered, she didn't need to pretend to smile and be okay. She let her features relax and kept her mind busy with taking notes. The classroom lights came on at the end of the period. Amelia put her passive mask back on and loaded her things back into her backpack.

The day's final bell rang, and she headed out the door, relieved the school day was over. Now she could go home and hide in her room. The hallway was crowded, and she joined in to be moved along as if with the tide. She immediately saw Damien to her left and moved over to avoid him.

"Hey, Amelia."

She cautiously turned to see Terrel beside her. They had the same history class together. He was nice, but he was friends with Damien.

"You want to go to the dance with me?"

Her eyes flew wide. Sure enough, she saw Damien and his crew standing behind Terrell, laughing.

Amelia felt the shock this time. She heard the sarcasm. Saw the sadistic glee of his friends. She'd thought Terrell was nice. Now he was here harassing her just like all the others.

She wanted to escape.

"Get away from me," she said hoarsely. Then she turned and ran. She took the nearest stairs. She didn't bother stopping at her locker and didn't pause until she pushed through the doors and exited outside. She took great gulps of air, trying to chase away the sobs. She walked slowly to the bus line, dreading that she had one last obstacle before she made it home.

"What's wrong?" Vashti hurried up beside her. "Are you heading home? Don't we have that extra band rehearsal tonight?"

"Oh, that's right. I forgot," Amelia said dully.

Now she had even longer before she made it home.

She reluctantly walked with Vashti back to the building.

"I don't know why you're so upset," Vashti chirped. "If a guy asked me to Homecoming, I'd be thrilled."

"What are you talking about?" Amelia's gaze swerved to her friend.

"I was right behind you in the hall when Terrell asked." Vashti opened the door, and Amelia stepped back into the school.

Amelia's embarrassment resurfaced. As if she hadn't felt enough humiliation. "He wasn't serious," she explained quietly. "He was just harassing me like everyone else."

"Oh, he was serious," Vashti insisted. "I've never heard you be so mean to someone. I think he felt bad. You should have seen his face after you took off."

Amelia shook her head. "He was teasing. His friends are always saying things like, "You want to go out with *her?*" Amelia was too humiliated to bear mentioning the lip-licking.

"It was for real, Amelia." Vashti's eyes were wide and honest. "He's nice and asked you to the dance. You said no. I think your exact words were, 'Get away from me.'"

Amelia cringed. The idea startled her. She'd never considered such a thing. It was impossible. Nevertheless, an awful feeling began to churn in her stomach, and she replayed the scene in her mind. For the first time, she considered what if.

What if Vashti was right? If Terrell had been serious—if he'd made a genuine request—then Amelia would have felt thrilled to say yes. No one had ever *really* asked her out.

If she'd blown off that invitation, Amelia would feel like the worst human ever.

No.

Terrell had asked her out as a joke for his friends' benefit. Hadn't he?

Chapter Six

Tayde

What's going on?

As soon as she stepped through the office door, Tayde saw that, once again, business was not as usual. The office was buzzing. People hurried every which way, and excitement lit the air as brightly as the fluorescent lights overhead.

This time she recognized the mood.

Something had happened, and that something had very likely happened to her column.

Gripping the tray of coffee cups tightly in her hand, she rushed straight to Frankie's cubicle.

"What's going on?" she asked urgently. "Something happened with my column, didn't it?"

Frankie lifted her hand and waved her on. "Don't pass 'Go.' Don't collect $200. Just go see Sheryl."

Suddenly, an awful thought gripped her. It had been over two months since her first column came out last summer. Though she'd posted numerous columns since then, they'd not heard from the mysterious Mr. Bells again. But if he'd responded this time....

"It's Mr. Bells, isn't it?" Tayde ventured. It was the only thing she could think of that would elicit the response she was seeing.

At the look on Frankie's face, Tayde felt her face pale. Her friend didn't say anything, but the panic and guilt in her expression were confirmation enough. Mr. Bells had struck again. Also clear—Tayde wouldn't like it at all.

"Let me take that," Frankie said, latching onto the tray of coffee cups held weakly in Tayde's hand.

"They gave me free coffee," she murmured distractedly.

"You don't like coffee," Frankie pointed out.

"No, but most people do."

"I'm most people. Thank you." Frankie set the entire tray of four grande coffee cups on her desk. "Now go see Sheryl."

Feeling an overwhelming sense of foreboding, Tayde left Frankie's cubicle and made her way to Sheryl's office.

She'd spent the morning doing a promotional visit at a coffee shop. After the success of her first column, Sheryl had decided Tayde's face was young and pretty enough to be *the* face of the magazine. Tayde Wright had become a small-time local celebrity. Though her subsequent columns hadn't gone viral like the first one, they'd still been popular. She'd kept to safe topics and had convinced herself that Mr. Bells was a one-hit wonder who wouldn't be heard from again. Numerous followers now became online subscribers, and advertisers were competing to do business with the magazine. While Tayde's columns weren't as sensational and ridiculous as Sheryl would prefer, she had been pleased. Until today.

Tayde stopped at the gray door, suddenly realizing she didn't want to face Sheryl unprepared again. She didn't want any surprises. She took out her phone and brought up social media.

She didn't want to look. She wanted to stick her head in the sand and wish it all away.

It only took a half second to find it. Feeling nauseated, she clicked on a headline that read: *Nice Guy meets Nice Girl*. She knew it would be bad, but that knowledge still didn't prepare her for the words addressed to her.

Dear Ms. Wright,

Please allow me to assure Nice Guy that there are nice girls in the world. In fact, I know of a nice girl at his school. She's smart and pretty. I think they even share some of the same classes.

Unfortunately, Nice Girl has not always been treated nicely. She's been bullied and harassed on a daily basis by supposedly nice guys at the school. These are guys that are popular and liked by both students and teachers, but when backs are turned, they can act like monsters.

And it's not just guys. Nice Girl often hides in the girls' locker room to escape the endless harassment. She hates lunch because it is another time when other students, like popular girls, target her with insults and teasing about her looks and even her food allergies.

But nothing is ever reported because Nice Girl thinks she would never be believed. It's all very subtle, almost untraceable, and unbelievable to those who assume popular equals nice. She wonders if maybe the harassment is normal after all, and maybe she's the problem.

On any given day, she is insulted and ridiculed by other girls at lunch. In the hallways, boys look at her and lick their lips suggestively. They also point her out to their friends and ask sarcastically, "Do you want to go out with her?"

What if, at the end of the day like this, a real nice guy were to legitimately ask her to a dance? After such harassment, do you think Nice Girl would believe him, or would she just assume his actions as further ridicule and want to escape as quickly as possible?

What is the greatest wrong here? Is it the wrong done to Nice Guy, who was hurt because he was rudely rejected? Or is it the wrong done to Nice Girl, who responded badly based on the harassment she endures? Who is the victim? Who is the villain?

Some may argue that the villains are the students who harass Nice Girl. And they are. But at some point, we are all a villain in someone's eyes. That doesn't excuse a person's poor choices or the consequences of those choices. But empathy offers an end to the cycle of hurting because you're hurt. Even the bullies have their own stories, and hopefully, they didn't realize what they did. I hope now they do.

When we know better, we can do better. The challenge is to increase the knowing. And when you can't know, assume the best. Find a new normal where we treat others with kindness, believing the best of them, even when their actions say differently. As you said, Ms. Wright, "we need to do better."

To Nice Guy, I have a message: Nice Girl sincerely apologizes for misinterpreting your request and is devastated that she hurt you. Should you choose to ask her again, she would very much like to say yes.

Can you hear the bells?

The gray door directly in front of Tayde opened.

"Are you coming in or not?" Sheryl demanded.

Tayde stepped into the office. "I was just reading Mr. Bells' comment," she hurriedly explained. "I saw you already gave it top billing and advertising." Her voice sounded almost normal despite the tremor in her hands.

"It's a work in progress." Sheryl brushed it off. "But we're at a point where we need to be on the same page."

Panic shot through her. Was she about to be fired?

Tayde quickly slipped into damage control mode. "I know. I'm really sorry. I had no idea about the girl. I can write a formal apology and—"

Sheryl held up her hand to stop her. "That's exactly what I don't want! That's why you're here. I was afraid you'd see Mr. Bells' letter, get emotional, and do something stupid. You are not to respond in any way. Write your next column."

"And why can't I respond?" Tayde asked boldly.

"Because we don't respond," Sheryl replied icily. "We don't apologize for our stories. We get reactions out of readers, which is what you did. You did nothing wrong. There's no way you could have known that girl's backstory."

"But he did," Tayde pointed out. Mr. Bells had done the work she hadn't.

Sheryl looked at Tayde, a superior brow cocked knowingly. "Only because she contacted him."

Tayde paused, confused. "What do you mean?"

"Come here," Sheryl motioned Tayde to come behind her desk for the first time. Tayde followed, noticing the cat perched in the center of Sheryl's desk like last time. Tayde crept up beside Sheryl, but remembering what happened last time, she took a wide berth around the cat. Sheryl moved aside to make room for Tayde, but she moved in the wrong direction, opening up the position between Sheryl and the cat on the desk. Seeing no other option, Tayde shot a wary glance at the cat and moved in position to see the computer screen.

Sheryl bent over the computer and made a few clicks, bringing up her original column in the *Wrongs Made Wright* series. As she worked, she explained, "A couple of days ago, right after your Nice Guy column came out, I got a new comment on Mr. Bells' first response to you, the one about the cemetery. I noticed because that one had died down a little, and the new comment shot it back up in rankings and visibility again. Of course, now it's back up even farther with more comments because of the renewed attention from the newest column, but this was the one from a few days ago."

Sheryl pointed at the screen.

Tayde bent over and looked. It was just one line and read:

`Mr. Bells, please contact me. I need your help.`

An email address was listed following the comment.

Tayde's mouth fell open. "You think that's her? That's Nice Girl?"

"Yes, I think it is," Sheryl said, her tone firm. "I'm guessing that Mr. Bells emailed her. She told him her story and wanted him to set the record straight—like he'd done with the cemetery. And he did. He hasn't responded in months. The only reason he did now is that he was asked."

"If that's her email address, then maybe I can call and apologize to her." Tayde took out her phone to copy down the email address.

Sheryl immediately shut off the screen. "Did you not hear me?" she hissed. "No apology! No contact with anyone involved with the cemetery or the Homecoming story. Understand?"

Tayde was done. She was tired, and her mind couldn't catch up to put brakes on her mouth. "No, I don't understand. Why? Please explain to me why I can't do the decent thing and make a personal apology to people I've hurt."

"Because you did nothing wrong." Unlike Tayde's voice, Sheryl's was calm and steady. "Because you were just doing your job. Because, as a representative of the magazine, an apology from you is the same as an apology from the magazine. We cannot accept any blame or liability under any circumstances. Because this interaction between you and Mr. Bells is now a thing that readers are invested in. Because I need all of your interactions to be in the public arena, and it won't move the story forward to go back and rehash old news. Because if you respond or contact him in any way, you might scare him into not responding again, and we can't have that! Are those enough reasons?"

"What do you mean we're a 'thing'?" Tayde asked, a little offended at the term. What was a "thing" anyway? Whatever it was, Tayde was sure she didn't want to be it, especially not with Mr. Bells.

Suddenly, she felt something brush along her back. She jerked away from it and whirled to see the cat standing and looking to rub against her back again. Sandwiched between Sheryl and the cat, Tayde couldn't move to get away from the cat's unwanted advances.

Completely clueless as to Tayde's discomfort, Sheryl navigated to the magazine's homepage and pointed to the menu. "I instructed Frankie to make a tab on the website dedicated to Wright vs. Mr. Bells, and we'll promote it as a thing. While you won't respond in writing to his comments, you will undoubtedly be asked about him during your promotional visits. You need to be very vague and provide only politically correct answers. No regret. No culpability."

The cat took another rub of his back against Tayde's shirt, and she distinctly heard a low purring. What was wrong with this cat? Tayde had thought it hated her. With each swipe past her, Tayde felt her skin crawl.

She tried to focus on Sheryl and on saying what was needed. She wasn't comfortable with the situation, and she wasn't simply referring to the cat's attention. Determinedly, she tried to explain, "I'm supposed to be righting wrongs. Yet I'm wronging others in the process. I don't know that I can continue to write these columns if I'm not permitted to do the right thing and respond when I've done a wrong!"

Sheryl sputtered in exasperation. "Tayde, your blasted integrity will prevent you from being the best writer you can be! If you need significance, look at all the good your columns have done, not as an individual but as part of a team. Without your letter and Mr. Bells' response, people wouldn't have known the full story behind the baseball game in the cemetery, and Nice Guy and Nice Girl would have assumed the worst of each other and never realized the story behind the other's actions. Now they have a chance."

Her words gave Tayde pause, and she realized Sheryl could be right. However, it still didn't sit well with her. This was not the way she strove to live her life. "But Mr. Bells doesn't know he's part of this 'team.'"

Sheryl straightened and put her hands on her hips. "Of course not. And we need to keep it that way. The more he responds, the better. But the fact that he doesn't respond to every column works to our advantage. People will follow because they never know when he might randomly post a zinger. You don't need to egg him on, but you can't scare him away."

Tayde didn't know how someone could be part of a team without even realizing he was a member. To her relief, the cat had taken his final sashay against her back and retreated to the center of the desk. Tayde crossed her arms across her front and turned her attention to the computer screen again. She felt sick over the words of Mr. Bells' letter still staring back at her.

"I still feel like I need to do *something*," she insisted. If she couldn't change her circumstances, maybe she could at least help someone else's. "That poor girl. The harassment needs to be reported to the school and stopped."

"Team Wright and Bells already took care of that," Sheryl assured brightly. "Do you have any idea how far this story has spread? It didn't go a little viral. Thousands and thousands of shares. I have networks calling and asking for interviews with you and contact information for Nice Guy and Nice Girl. I refused all offers. And I hid Nice Girl's comment on the original column from public viewing. I didn't want anyone else making the connection and contacting her. I don't think either Nice Guy or Nice Girl would appreciate their anonymity being compromised. People who contact us need to feel confident that we are safe and won't reveal personal information."

Sheryl's words could almost be classified as nice, and Tayde appreciated that approach to reader input. But the letters had been addressed to her. She still wished she could make that personal connection.

"There's a story there, Ms. Sutton," Tayde said, trying to offer a carrot Sheryl would find tempting while also getting her what she wanted. "If I contacted Nice Guy and Nice Girl, I could find out the next chapter and report if they went to Homecoming together. Readers would like that."

Sheryl scrunched up her mouth in distaste as if she'd just gotten a whiff of garbage. "That's not our story, Tayde. Or maybe I should say, *they* are not our story. If we report a happy ending, readers will be satisfied and tune out. The story is you, Mr. Bells, and the interaction of how he responds to you."

But I'm not allowed to respond to him.

Sheryl narrowed her eyes as if assessing her, and Tayde tried not to squirm under the intense gaze. "I haven't yet decided if I'll accept any television interviews on your behalf," she mused. "Let's give it a little more time. If you interview now, they'll want to know about Nice Guy and Nice Girl, and we can't provide information. Mr. Bells responded this time because he was asked. If he responds again, the networks will want to know about you and him—that's the story we want to draw people in."

Sheryl was like a master chess player. She had a set, uncompromising strategy, and she was fine about sacrificing lesser pieces to achieve her overall plan.

"How do you even know Mr. Bells is a mister?" Tayde asked with a touch of irritability. She suddenly wondered what information Sheryl was hiding from her.

"I don't know," Sheryl answered easily. "I'm just assuming. It makes for a better story if it's a guy responding. And I don't intend to peek behind the curtain to find out for sure."

She abruptly moved aside for Tayde to pass back to the other side of the desk. "That's all for now," she announced crisply. "I need your next column for Monday. Enjoy your weekend. Keep your head down and your lips sealed with all of the publicity."

Tayde nodded, though she still didn't feel good about the situation.

"You're doing well, Tayde," Sheryl called to her as Tayde walked to the office door. "I have big plans for the magazine, and I intend to include you in them."

The words should have thrilled her, but they didn't. Instead, she felt defeated. She dutifully turned back around. "Thanks, Ms. Sutton. I'll have the new column ready."

Tayde's eyes fell on the cat on his throne across the room, and her hazel eyes connected with his yellow ones. Then he opened his mouth just a bit and revealed his sharp fangs.

Sheryl had already turned her computer back to her computer screen, and Tayde was only too happy to make haste away from Sheryl and her psychotic feline.

After leaving Sheryl's office, Tayde didn't return directly to her cubicle. Instead, she ducked back into Frankie's. More than half of the staff were on lunch break. Hopefully, she could steal a few minutes to decompress with her friend before everyone returned.

Frankie immediately twirled in her chair to face Tayde and eagerly questioned, "How did it go?"

Feeling grumpy, Tayde scooted up to sit on the table beside Frankie's computer. "Oh, Sheryl's very happy," she assured. "She's over the moon at the idea of tying my body to a post in the public square so everyone can ridicule me. Just as long as the social media post gets a lot of likes."

"Wow, that's dramatic and morbid," Frankie said in awe. "I like it. Totally in favor. I'll make a tab for it on the website."

Tayde raised an eyebrow. "Right beside the Wright vs. Mr. Bells tab?"

Frankie had the decency to look sheepish. "You know I didn't have a choice."

"Frankie, did you read that letter?" she moaned, putting her head in her hands. "I'm so humiliated!"

"He wrote your pants off," Frankie agreed.

"He totally did! And I deserved it!"

Frankie shook her head and reached over to grab a bag of

cheese puffs. "There's no way you could have known any of that, Tayde. Give yourself a break." She popped one in her mouth and started chewing.

"I just wish I could contact him," Tayde said miserably, "I'd like to apologize, but I'd also like to just talk to him. I'd rather not be one-upped again. But that's not what Sheryl wants. She likes the interaction and how he proves T. Wright wrong."

With a puff held delicately in her fingers, Frankie mused, "Do you notice he always addresses you as Ms. Wright, not T. Wright? It's like he knew who you were even before you started making public appearances. Now it's not as big of a deal. Most people know you're a woman, but when he first called you Ms. Wright, you were only known as T. Wright, and we hadn't even released a bio."

"Gah, you're right!" Tayde exclaimed, realizing the different use of names for the first time. "I'm sure he looked me up, and it's not like I've been hiding. But I can't look him up! Frankie, I have to find him!"

"How?" she asked in between munching. "He says nothing personal about himself. He only ever advocates for others."

Yes, she was right, and it was maddening. She was trying to find the Robin Hood of the writing world. Even worse was the realization that she was in the role of the Sheriff of Nottingham. But she didn't want to be painted as the villain for trying to catch him! She had to stop this madness.

Trying to focus, she reached out and stole one of Frankie's cheese puffs, hoping a little munching might help. "Obviously, he's a writer," she mused aloud. "I mean, seriously. These aren't ordinary writing skills. The way he tells a story... the pace of it... his tone. He's a writer."

Tayde popped the cheese puff in her mouth and instantly regretted it. It tasted like cheese-flavored cardboard, but not even the good kind of cheese. She could almost taste the chemicals—like plastic, but less healthy.

While Tayde gagged, Frankie paid her no mind and eagerly joined in on the investigation. "And you know he's a—pardon the term—'nice guy.' You wrote a column throwing a sexual harassment victim under the bus. He could have torn you to shreds. But he didn't. He's not mean. He's respectful. He was even nice to those awful bullies!"

Tayde couldn't clear the debris out of her throat. Desperately, she swiped the water bottle beside Frankie, not even caring that she may be drinking after someone else. To her, it was an emergency, and she didn't want to die at the hands of a cheese puff.

The entire time Tayde tried to hack out a lung, Frankie calmly continued popping the cheese puffs into her mouth.

The water helped, and Tayde finally could breathe. Eyes watering, she ventured an idea. "Maybe he's a pastor. He'd have to be nice if he was a pastor. And he might have decent writing skills."

"Nah, I don't think he's a pastor," Frankie disagreed. "Preachers tend to speak more than they write. If he were a pastor, he'd roast you from the pulpit on a Sunday morning."

Tayde sighed, both for her hopeless situation and the sight of Frankie continuing to eat the toxic orange puffs. How could she eat those things?

"So, how am I going to find him?" Tayde asked helplessly.

Frankie tossed the empty bag into a trash can and stuck her finger in her mouth while she thought. She brought the finger out, minus the orange dust. Then she grabbed a napkin and cleaned the rest of her fingers. She followed it up with a squirt of hand sanitizer before turning back to her computer. Tayde was just so thankful the cheese puff episode was over and hadn't involved the enjoyment of licking each finger.

Completely clueless about her friend's disgust, Frankie focused on her computer and typed in a password to gain access. "You're on your own with that. I can throw out wild theories, but I can't help you locate him."

Tayde lowered her voice to a whisper, not wanting anyone who remained in the office to overhear. "But you could trace his IP address."

Frankie turned and leveled her with a glare that would make a saint flinch.

"I don't intend to show up on his doorstep," Tayde hastened to explain. "I just need a way to contact him."

Frankie turned back to her computer as she spoke casually. "You wouldn't need to trace his IP address to do that. The website requires anyone who comments to provide an email address. Sheryl wanted it set up that way so we could send website visitors a zillion spam emails a day until they become subscribers. As an admin, if Sheryl looks at the comments on the website, she can click on the commenter's name, and it will show the provided email address."

"But he could have used a fake email address," Tayde pointed out, unsure whether or not Frankie was providing helpful information.

Frankie shrugged. "Possible."

Tayde sighed, "But it's the only lead I have. Aren't you an admin too? Can you get me the email address he provided?"

"Nope," Frankie said flatly. "Not interested in getting fired. Sheryl forbade you from contacting him, correct?"

"Pretty much," Tayde said miserably. Then why had Frankie even mentioned the email addresses?

Frankie turned and faced Tayde directly. She peered over her glasses and met Tayde's gaze, her eyes serious. Speaking slowly and deliberately, she said, "So any information can't come through me. You have to get it on your own."

Tayde rolled her eyes in frustration. "And how do I do that?"

Frankie turned back to her computer. "Oh, drat! My computer screen locked me out again. I hate that. If I don't touch my keyboard for thirty seconds, the screen locks, and then I have to reenter my password. Maybe I should adjust my settings like Sheryl had me adjust hers. If she steps away from her computer, the screen doesn't lock for a minute and thirty seconds. I thought that was too long, but that's the way she wanted it. Oh, look! It's almost lunchtime for the second shift."

Frankie's words suddenly clicked, and Tayde's eyes grew round. Not everyone went to lunch at the same time. Sheryl hadn't wanted the office to completely close for the lunch hour, so employees were divided into shifts. Tayde and Frankie were part of the second shift. More importantly, Sheryl usually took her lunch break with the second shift.

A wild, crazy idea slowly formed in Tayde's mind.

"Since we've been sitting here chatting, I'm going to work a few minutes into lunch," Frankie told Tayde. "Sheryl wanted me to send her a report of the post stats so far."

"Okay," Tayde responded. Though her heart was beating in excitement, her words sounded casual. "I'll get a little work done too. Do you want to give me a call when you're ready? Then we can grab a sandwich."

"Sure, I can do that," Frankie agreed.

Tayde went back to her desk and checked her email. The number of new messages was daunting. Sheryl wasn't exaggerating about this being a big deal.

In the quiet office, her ears caught the sound she'd been waiting for. A door closed. Tayde turned her body slightly so she could see the entrance to her cubicle out of the corner of her eye.

Sure enough, a few seconds later, Sheryl's heels clicked by. As soon as she passed, Tayde jumped up to peer around the edge of the partition, watching until Sheryl turned the corner toward the front door.

Then Tayde took off in the other direction. She walked quickly, unafraid of being seen. The restroom was across from Sheryl's office, so her rushing off in that direction could be easily explained.

Was she really doing this?

One minute, thirty seconds. That's all the time Frankie said she had.

But she didn't give herself time to answer that question. *Don't think. Just get it done!*

And she didn't. She didn't think if it was right or wrong. She didn't anticipate what would happen if she was caught. She didn't let her conscience let her second guess what she was doing. She didn't consult anyone but the impulse of the moment. She simply saw a fleeting opportunity and jumped on it.

Reaching Sheryl's office door, she looked both ways before slowly turning the knob and pushing it open. She kept the tension on the knob while she turned around, closing it with barely a whisper of sound.

That's the moment when she realized she'd made a mistake. Only when she turned around did she remember the room had a witness. Even with Sheryl gone, her cat still perched calmly on his throne.

But she'd come this far, and she wasn't letting the yellow glare of a disapproving cat stop her.

Had she made it in time?

She made a wide arc around the desk, feeling relief at the sight of the glowing computer screen. The cat turned his head and watched her every move, but she ignored him. She stayed out of his reach and angled the screen away from him.

Tayde liked cats. She'd had an orange kitty named Ronald Reagan growing up. She'd wanted a kitten so badly, and her dad had finally given permission, provided he be allowed to name it. Ronald Reagan was the best cat ever. Even dad had admitted that the cat had lived up to his name. But now, she cast a wary glance at Sheryl's tuxedo-clad cat and decided she preferred her cats to be moderately sane.

Seeing that the cat appeared stable and still, she turned her attention to the computer. She wasn't quite sure what to look for, but the magazine's website was already open in a window on the screen. She quickly navigated to her post about Nice Guy. Then she scrolled down to the comments. Finding the one made by Mr. Bells, she clicked the blank avatar. To her delight, a bunch of stats came up on the screen. In that information, an email was listed. Tayde wanted a piece of paper and a pen to write it down but didn't dare take anything but information. Thankfully, it was a simple email. She took a mental picture and memorized it.

The pocket of Tayde's cardigan suddenly began vibrating. She drew out her phone, and her heart leaped at Frankie's name on the screen.

She swiped her finger to answer, but it was so slick with sweat that she couldn't get it to respond until the third try. "Hello?" she hissed into the phone.

"I'm ready for lunch! Like right now!" Frankie said brightly. Then came the fierce whisper, "She's here! Get out!"

"She's here?" Tayde's shrill whisper sent electricity through the office. "How is she here?"

"Hi, Sheryl," Frankie's voice was loud and dramatic, but it was as if it were coming from a distance—like she'd left the phone on while she'd sprinted to cut Sheryl off. "I was wondering. What all do you want on the page dedicated to Wright versus Mr. Bells?"

Tayde ended the call and turned to the door. At that exact instant, the cat jumped off the desk and landed right beside her. Tayde let out a strangled shriek and lifted her feet, dancing around to avoid the cat. But the cat looked up at her innocently, seeming to only desire to rub affectionately around her legs.

Tayde leaped over him and sprinted for the door. Five steps later, her hand enclosed around the knob. She turned it, but the smooth metal slipped in her grasp. She brought her other hand forward and gripped the knob with both hands.

Dear Lord! I shouldn't be here!

Desperately, she turned. The door opened, and she slipped out. She turned around and glimpsed the cat jump back up on the desk and level a hateful glare in her direction. She knew that crazy cat would tell on her.

A fraction of a second after the door made a soft bump closed behind her, she caught movement in her peripheral vision. Sheryl turned the corner with Tayde in full view.

She'd been caught!

Not knowing what else to do, she kept her gaze on the door, lifted her fist, and knocked.

"Did you need something?" Sheryl's crisp question broke the silence.

Tayde's startled jump wasn't an act. "Oh, yes. I thought... I was just wondering..." Her mind fumbled frantically before latching onto a coherent thought. "My inbox is loaded with invitations for interviews, requests for comments, and messages from principals wanting to know if the incidents in the column occurred at their high school. How do you want me to respond?"

"Don't. Or if you have to, simply reply, 'No comment.'

Forward me any legitimate offers or anything that looks vitally important."

Tayde nodded, struggling to find a way to continue the conversation. She needed to stall Sheryl for one minute and thirty seconds, or she'd see that the computer screen, which should have been locked several minutes ago, was still active.

"And what about the library event I'm supposed to attend this afternoon?" she asked, grasping at anything to fill the space. "Do you want me to keep that?" It wasn't a question she'd planned on asking Sheryl. Tayde had already committed to going to the library. She couldn't back out now.

"That should be tame enough. Just remember—" Sheryl offered her hand as if waiting for Tayde to fill in the blank.

"No comment," Tayde supplied. Sheryl turned the knob and opened her office door. Tayde had nothing else to keep her. Hopefully, enough time had elapsed for the computer screen to revert to black.

"Good girl." Sheryl purred before shutting the door behind her.

But Tayde didn't feel good at all. She'd just gone behind her boss's back to sneak into her office and steal an email address she wasn't supposed to have.

Even worse, she'd succeeded.

Chapter Seven

A knock sounded at the door. Tayde set her laptop on the couch beside her and stood to answer it. She wasn't expecting anyone, and it was too late on a Saturday night for a package delivery.

As far as she knew, Knox wasn't expecting anyone either. His dates never came to the apartment. Knox had played a game of basketball with friends and was now showering so he could go out later. Tayde had no doubt he'd be gone until the wee hours of the morning again.

After looking through the peephole, Tayde immediately opened the door, surprised to see Frankie standing on her doorstep. "Frankie, what are you doing here?"

"Surprise!" she said brightly. "I brought you a pumpkin pie!"

Frankie breezed in with the pie, and Tayde shut the door behind her.

Tayde frowned. She didn't even like pumpkin pie. She

thought Frankie knew that.

"Did someone say pumpkin pie?" Knox entered the room, still toweling off his wet hair. "My favorite!"

Frankie set the pie on the counter. "Can I get you a slice, Knox?" she asked shyly.

"Sure!" he readily accepted. "Always have time for pie."

Frankie cut a slice, placed it on a dish, and slid it across the counter to Knox. She didn't even bother to ask Tayde if she wanted any.

Tayde watched Frankie curiously. "You're always welcome, Frankie. But why did you come by?"

"Pie. Isn't it obvious?" Knox said around mouthfuls. "This is delicious, Frankie."

Frankie blushed.

Tayde didn't think she'd ever seen Frankie blush, and she'd had no idea her friend knew how to turn on the oven, let alone bake a pie.

"You had a rough week," Frankie explained. "I wanted to check on you and find out if you'd heard anything back from the email you sent."

Tayde frowned. She knew exactly what Frankie was talking about, and her friend would be disappointed. "I haven't sent anything yet."

"Why not?" Frankie protested. "You went through all that effort of sneaking into Sheryl's office and stealing—"

"You did what?" Knox asked, freezing with his mouth full of pie.

Frankie readily supplied, "She snuck into our boss's office and stole an email address she wasn't supposed to know about. And she almost got caught!"

Knox looked at her with both shock and admiration gleaming from his brown eyes. "Tayde, I can't believe you did that! I'm kinda proud. Shocked. A little bit worried about my own security. But proud."

Frankie giggled loudly.

It was funny, but it *wasn't* that funny.

A lightbulb went off, and Tayde looked from Frankie's flushed, smiling face to Knox and back again. Did Frankie *like* Knox?

The idea was crazy. Tayde remembered all the times they'd all attended church activities together. Knox was usually surrounded by flirting girls, and Frankie usually held back and watched the scene disdainfully. She'd never said anything about liking Knox. But it certainly looked like she was trying to flirt with him and doing a very awkward job of it.

Frankie was brilliant, funny, and direct. But she had some difficulty associating with lesser beings. She didn't seem to know how to react in some social situations, and Tayde couldn't recall her dating at all. She just needed to find a great guy who saw her for the treasure she was. Unfortunately, she didn't know that her brother was that kind of wonderful.

She studied her brother, her initial excitement now chased away by doubts. Knox had terrible taste in women. Frankie was entirely too smart and independent and wasn't the bombshell model type Knox usually went for.

But Frankie would be good for him, and Knox would be good for her.

She watched Knox's handsome face as he ate his pie. She noticed the glances Frankie sent in his direction. However, he was completely clueless.

"Thanks for the pie, Frankie," he said. He set his plate in the sink and grabbed his jacket. "I gotta run. Don't want to keep my date waiting."

At no point did Knox even glance Frankie's way. Tayde felt a wave of hopelessness. Knox would never be interested in her. Tayde knew her friend would get hurt, and there was nothing she could do about it.

Knox left, and Frankie snapped back to her normal self. She perched on a barstool and leveled a look of reproach at Tayde. "So why didn't you send a message to the forbidden email after you went to all the work to get it?"

Tayde walked over and flopped down on the couch. "I feel so guilty about going behind Sheryl's back to get it. I haven't quieted my conscience enough to go through with sending a message."

Frankie stood and stowed the rest of the pumpkin pie in the refrigerator before joining Tayde on the couch. "Tayde, those letters were written for you. Talk about *Wrongs Made Wright*. It's wrong to not allow you to contact someone who contacted you."

Unfortunately, Tayde was learning that everyone has a different definition of "right." And she didn't know what the true right in this situation was. Was it right to respond to a letter addressed to her in an attempt to apologize for a hurt she inadvertently caused, or was it more right to follow her boss's orders? "But if I contact him and it doesn't go well, I could face some serious consequences. If Sheryl finds out, I'll be fired."

"Yes, that could happen. It's your choice. Mr. Bells went a long time without responding to one of your columns. He might not respond again. Are you okay with never talking to him, apologizing, or knowing who he is? Are you fine with not contacting him even though his email address now lives in your mind?" Frankie looked at her with one eyebrow raised.

Frankie knew that Tayde was not okay with those possibilities.

"Maybe," Tayde said defensively.

Frankie patted Tayde's knee in a patronizing gesture and stretched. "Good luck with that!" She stretched. "I'm going to head out. I have a date with a shower and a good book tonight."

"And I have a date with a column that's due to Sheryl by

tomorrow," Tayde grumbled. "Have I mentioned how much I hate that the column is published on Mondays? Hopefully, I can get it done tonight and still have my Sunday free."

Frankie stood. "That's not going to change anytime soon. Sheryl depends on the popularity of your column to carry the magazine through the rest of the week. The rest of the content is coming along, but your column has more page views than anything else we publish, and it's nowhere close. Your column from a month ago will still get more attention than this week's current articles."

"Reading how someone makes me look like a fool is disturbingly popular." Tayde stood with Frankie and began repositioning the pillows on the couch and picking up the trash Knox had left earlier. Anything was better than facing her computer screen and the work in front of her.

Frankie reached down and moved one of the pillows so it was off-center. "Yes, it is. And I have the data to back it up. Honestly, Tayde, people are tuning into your columns just to see if Bells will respond."

"Which means Sheryl will want him to continue to respond and make me look bad," Tayde filled in. She knew Frankie had moved the pillow just to mess with her, but without comment, she moved it back to sit in the corner at just the right angle.

Frankie shrugged. "If you want different..."

She didn't have to finish the thought. Tayde's mind filled it in for her. *You have to do different.*

"Don't you want to take your pie home?" Tayde asked as her friend headed to the door.

"That's okay. I'll leave it for Knox."

Tayde thought about questioning Frankie about Knox, but she decided she didn't want to know. She had enough stress and didn't want to take on the worry of the broken heart surely awaiting her friend.

Frankie left, and Tayde took out her laptop. She'd already selected a letter and started responding to it. She did her best to block out everything else and complete the task. It was easier than she'd anticipated, and before the clock struck midnight, she made her final edits for the column.

As she read it through one last time, she bit her lip worriedly, trying to anticipate any stray thread Mr. Bells might latch onto. Had she missed something? Was this a topic that would spark his interest? Could anyone be offended by what she'd written?

But the answers to her questions remained elusive, and her thoughts spun into a hurricane of worried chaos that only intensified. Realizing she wouldn't get satisfactory answers, she attached the column to an email and sent it to Sheryl.

Now it was done, and too late to change anything.

Feeling weary, she showered and readied for bed. She climbed into bed and waited for sleep to overtake her, but the hurricane of thoughts still raged.

It was too late to change her column, but it wasn't too late to try to prevent a response from Mr. Bells. The stolen email address repeated through her mind like the steady rhythm of a drum.

If you want different, you have to do different.

Tayde sat up in bed and opened her laptop. She brought up her personal email and typed in the stolen address she'd memorized.

Quickly, she wrote,

Hello, this is Tayde Wright. Chronicle will not allow me to publicly (or privately) contact you. I am making this personal contact myself without my company's knowledge or consent. Please convey to the Paulsen family and "Nice Girl" my heartfelt apologies. I had no idea of their stories before your letter, and I was not allowed to do research before responding to the reader letters. It bothers me that others were hurt by my column. Though the magazine is happy with the popularity you have brought with your responses, I am personally quite humiliated to be made the fool.

If you wish to discuss these stories or any of my future columns, please call me at the number below. Feel free to call anytime.

My job requires me to continue to respond to reader letters. Can you please tell me if you intend to continue to respond to my columns?

Tayde pushed the send button before she could second-guess herself. She felt a thrill of exhilaration followed quickly by stark fear.

What had she done? What if Mr. Bells contacted the magazine and got her in trouble? What if her email egged him into responding more, not less?

She closed the laptop and set it on her nightstand. Flopping back on her bed, she pulled her pillow over her head with a groan. She might feel even worse than she did before sending the email.

She wasn't going to sleep tonight.

A soft beep sent her sitting straight up in bed. She recognized the notification sound of an incoming email.

Snatching her laptop again, she opened the machine's screen that hadn't quite put itself to sleep before the incoming email hit Tayde's inbox.

Mr. Bells had replied.

She clicked the message at the top of the list and held her breath. It was only one line, the five little words creating a pit of dread in Tayde's stomach.

Depends on what you write.

The Bells of Christmas

Dear Ms. Wright,

Never in my life have I regretted a good deed. Until today.

An acquaintance of mine posted on social media that she did not have food to feed her children lunch. I don't know this woman well, but my heart went out to her. I know she's had a difficult time holding a job and that she and her boyfriend lost their rental house and are now living in an RV.

I messaged her and told her I'd bring her some groceries. I also asked if her family had any food allergies. Then I went to the store and loaded up on staples. I got bread, milk, peanut butter, fried chicken, fruit, and vegetables. I even put in a package of cookies for the kids. I took everything straight from the store to the RV park and arrived at about 2:00 in the afternoon.

She wasn't there when I arrived, but her boyfriend was. I knocked on the door of a 1970s relic of a motorhome. A man in boxer shorts and a tank top opened the door with one hand. His other hand was busy holding a cigarette. As soon as he opened the door, three tiny dogs started barking. I set the stacks of groceries on the filthy brown carpet, never stepping inside myself. I glimpsed a sack of dog food and a 1970's brown décor, but not much else.

The man nodded and shut the door on the yapping dogs. I was on my way, feeling shocked by the whole experience.

If they didn't have enough money to buy food to feed their children lunch, how did they have enough money to buy cigarettes and food for their dogs?

Is it wrong for me to be upset? I just spent a load of money buying groceries for them, while they spent a load of money buying cigarettes! Had I just been conned? I certainly felt like it!

There is so much legitimate need in this world, but shouldn't people help themselves instead of depending solely on others? I feel like I just enabled these people to continue their bad choices and unhealthy lifestyle. Was it my fault for being naïve?

I am hoping you can help let people know that before asking for charity from others for their basic needs, they should take a hard look at what is non-basic and what they can do for themselves. Maybe it sounds harsh, but someone unwilling to work and unable to feed their children should not be buying cigarettes and feeding pets. Get a job, quit smoking, and find your pets a loving home that is more able to support their needs while you attend to your own.

Maybe my example will help others know that before they rush off to do a good deed, they should make sure they are not being taken advantage of. It's just sad that experiences like this make generosity less likely. I know I won't be so quick to respond to someone's plea for help, and that's sad. But as they say. "Fool me once, shame on you. Fool me twice, shame on me."

I won't be a fool again.

Sincerely,
Regretting a Good Deed

Dear Duped Do-Gooder,

First, let me applaud you for your beautiful heart in wanting to help those in need. You probably feel very taken advantage of, and you should. Unfortunately, your experience is not unusual. It's a problem in our society. On a personal level, before people ask for a handout, they should do everything they can with their own hands first. And that includes removing the cigarette from the fingers. Prioritizing cigarettes over providing food for your children is inexcusable.

We live in a day and age where anyone can make a heartbreaking digital plea for charity. Funding requests can come for many different reasons, and many of those reasons are legitimate. But asking for help often ends up being easier than doing the work to help yourself. Taking a scroll on social media will earn you multiple pleas for money in the space of a minute, and the risk is that we get desensitized to it. Because there is so much fraud and so much entitlement in the world, it becomes difficult to spot worthy causes.

I don't know the answer, but it seems to be getting worse. Are those who get assistance from others more likely to become dependent on that assistance? Will your acquaintance message you directly next time she says they are out of food? The danger is a scenario where people can make more money by claiming it from government assistance and charitable sources than by working. Then there is no motivation or reason to work. All that is left is a sense of entitlement that they are receiving what they need and deserve.

So, if you're considering asking for help, please ensure you've helped yourself first. Eliminate the unnecessaries to fund your necessary.

If you're thinking about giving help, please do. But be wise in your generosity, careful not to further dependency or entitlement, but let your gift be a blessing where it is truly needed.

Generosity is right. Taking advantage of that generosity is wrong. Please do not grow weary doing good, but let your good find the right object.

Sincerely,
T. Wright

Carole

Carole shut the door on the last empty cupboard. It made a solid *thunk* as it connected to the thin particle board of the rest of the cupboards. She'd checked them all and found nothing.

She took one step over to the small refrigerator and opened it again to stare inside at the empty shelves, wishing something—anything—would magically appear.

But a can of beer was the fridge's only occupant, and she couldn't feed that to her children for lunch.

With one more step, she was beside the bed. She sat down and stared unseeing at the small motorhome around her. Her two boys were watching TV on the couch, but she paid them no mind.

How did she get here? In this RV... at this moment... with not a shred of food to feed her children for lunch.

Her three dogs hopped on the bed beside her, fighting for seating on her lap. Carole snuggled them, taking the little comfort they offered.

Carole sighed, unable to identify one isolated incident or bad decision that caused her to arrive on this day. Rather, it was a series of bad luck. If only they hadn't hated her and tried so hard to get her fired at her last fast-food job, she would have her own money and not have to depend on Hank. If only the landlords at the apartment complex hadn't found out about her dogs, they would still have their place and not be living in this 1978 motorhome. Carole suspected her neighbor had turned them in. Yes, it was against the rules to have dogs in the apartment, but if she could have only made them understand that she needed her dogs, they wouldn't have kicked them out. Her dogs loved her unconditionally and never asked her to do anything other than love them in return.

But now she had her dogs but no place to live and no food. It was a complete myth that living in an RV park was cheaper. Staying here was more expensive than their rent at the apartment, and it took every little bit Hank brought home.

The door to the motorhome opened, and Hank walked in.

"Home already?" Carole called.

"Yep, no work today. Maybe tomorrow," Hank replied. He walked over to the fridge, opened it, and took out the lonely can of beer. He stripped off his work clothes and then walked back over to the TV.

"Go play," he told the boys, brushing them off the couch. With a grunt, he sprawled on the ratty couch and opened his beer.

Carole felt panic well up inside of her. Hank worked for a

company delivering porta potties. It was a good job and paid good money, but if there were no porta potties to deliver, Hank didn't work. He said his company was promising to give him more duties. He didn't want to clean the porta potties, but they were talking about delivering to new areas. But it hadn't happened yet.

"Carole, can you deal with them already?" Hank asked irritably. "I can't hear the TV!"

Carole blinked back to the present, realizing her boys were wrestling on the floor while the dogs jumped around, yipping their cheers.

Carole stood. "Boys, knock it off! Why don't you go on down to the park and leave Hank alone?" The park was a couple of blocks away, but since the boys were eleven and nine, Carole sent them down there all the time to play.

"But I'm hungry, Mom," eleven-year-old Sterling whined.

"Me too," echoed nine-year-old Calvin.

"No snacks right now. After you go to the park, we'll have some lunch," she assured.

They whined their way out the door, leaving Carole to wonder exactly how she'd keep her promise of lunch.

Hank lit a cigarette. She hated that he smoked. But he earned the money. She couldn't object to how he spent it. She and the kids depended on him for the scraps he threw their way.

She wished she could change things, but she couldn't. No job, no education, nobody else to take care of her, and two kids to feed. She was trapped. As long as Hank tolerated her, the kids, and her dogs, she'd stay and be grateful for him. She didn't have a choice.

Choking on the cigarette smoke, she tried to open one of the aged sliding windows, but it wouldn't budge. Hank didn't move to help. His eyes stayed glued on the TV, exactly where they'd be for the rest of the day. He wouldn't help with the kids. If he got hungry, he'd head out and get himself something to eat. She didn't know what money he used, but he always seemed to find enough funds for cigarettes.

She was on her own. She sat on the bed and took out her phone. Not knowing what else to do, she brought up her social media account and wrote a post.

```
I have no food for lunch for my kids. No money.
```

She felt embarrassed to post something. She didn't want to beg. But maybe if she didn't come out and ask, someone would volunteer. Deciding she had no other idea, she posted and waited to see if someone would respond.

Sure enough, someone posted almost immediately telling her the locations of the local food boxes. But Carole had checked the one closest to her yesterday. That's where she'd gotten the can of soup they'd eaten for dinner last night. She'd already taken the meager offerings, and she already knew there was nothing left. But she didn't want to explain all of that, so she just stayed silent, watching the screen.

Suddenly her phone sounded with the notification of an incoming message. She quickly read it.

```
Hi, Carole. I saw your post. Do you still need
food? If so, I can run to the store and get you
some bread, milk, and a few other things. Does your
family have any allergies?
```

Carole's face blushed with embarrassment. The person who had replied wasn't someone she considered a friend. She'd gone to school with her, but they'd never been more than acquaintances. They hadn't spoken since Carole had dropped out.

She was so ashamed. But she did what she needed and replied simply.

```
Yes food. No allergies.
```

The woman asked where to bring the food, and Carole gave her the address of the RV park and their lot number. Over the next thirty minutes, a few others commented on the locations of food boxes, food pantries, or where she could apply for government assistance. One person commented, "Sorry." But nobody else offered to help.

Her phone beeped with an incoming message.

```
On my way.
```

Carole felt ill. She didn't know that she could face the humiliation. What could she say? This woman would see her old, run-down RV and know that she was a complete failure at life.

She heard a car engine.

"Hank!" she whispered urgently. "A woman is dropping off some food. Take the food and tell her I'm not here."

Hank grunted. Carole didn't know if he'd even heard her, but she didn't wait. She crawled into the bed and curled up in the corner. Quickly, she piled all the blankets on top of herself and hoped her hiding place would work.

A knock sounded at the door.

Hank hefted himself up and trudged to open it. The dogs immediately began yapping so furiously that Carole had to strain to hear.

"Hi, I'm looking for Carole," a woman's voice said.

"She ain't here," Hank said. "Must be taking the boys

somewhere."

"Okay," she said. "I guess I can just leave this food here. Will that work?"

Carole didn't hear Hank's response, but she heard grunting and the sound of rustling plastic. She imagined the grocery sacks being placed on the threadbare brown carpet.

She heard no more conversation, but the door slammed shut. The dogs calmed down, and she thought she heard the car outside drive away.

She cautiously parted the blankets so she could breathe the smoke-filled air. Hearing nothing but the sound of the TV, she crawled across the bed and peered down the length of the motorhome. Hank was once again sprawled across the couch, and multiple plastic grocery bags cluttered the floor between them.

She stood and began sorting through them. Quickly, tears filled her eyes. The sacks didn't just contain a few items for lunch. There was enough food to last them several days. In her humiliation, Carole felt another emotion—gratefulness. The woman had been virtually a stranger, yet she'd been so very generous, providing more than Carole had asked or hoped. Carole quickly stowed the groceries in the fridge and the cupboards. They'd eat the fried chicken for dinner tonight. For lunch, she'd make the boys peanut butter and jelly sandwiches.

"Anything good in there?" Hank asked.

"Just regular food," Carole responded vaguely.

Not satisfied with her report, Hank stood and came to survey the selection himself.

"Not a very good friend," he muttered. "No chips or nothing."

Spotting a package of cookies, Hank confiscated it and headed back to the couch, where he immediately opened it and began eating.

Carole wished she'd grabbed a couple of the cookies out for the boys, but it was too late now.

She'd just finished cutting two sandwiches in half when the door jerked open for the boys to enter. She made them sit at the tiny table and put their lunch in front of them. She also poured glasses of milk.

"These are good," Sterling said, plopping a grape into his mouth.

Carole didn't remember the last time they'd had fruit. Fresh fruit wasn't something she could pick up in one of the food boxes.

"What are these?" Calvin asked, holding up a carrot like it was something from another planet.

"Those are carrots," Carole answered.

Calvin thoughtfully took a bite and chewed.

"I like them," He announced. "I think we have them at school sometimes."

With Hank on the couch and the kids at the table, there wasn't another place to sit, so Carole stood and watched them eat, feeling a strange sense of satisfaction. She didn't know what they'd do when the food ran out in a few days. She didn't know how they'd pay for their RV space at the end of the week. She didn't know what she'd do if Hank decided he was done with her.

But for today, her kids were eating. And for just a moment, she felt like a good mom.

Chapter Nine

Tayde

Tayde knew it was a nightmare. She knew she was asleep and that what was happening wasn't real. But she couldn't wake herself and make it stop.

She'd been here before.

She was trapped, trying to fight off sleep, but it was as if shadows clung to her, suffocating her and pulling her back down into the abyss. She couldn't escape.

She could hear voices, though she couldn't see who was speaking. They were loud and echoed as if from a distance.

"There's nothing wrong with her... No medical reason... She has psychological issues... Even the nurses noticed and said something about it."

She recognized the murmur of her mother's voice, but she couldn't hear the words.

She was drowning. She had to breathe. She tried to raise herself out of the dark water. She opened her mouth to cry and defend herself, but no sound came. The muscles of her raw throat ached with strain.

The loud voice came again. "She needs psychological help. We can admit her today to a psychiatric hospital. Therapy... medication... It's what she needs."

No! Please, no! her mind screamed. *Mom, don't leave me! Someone, please believe me! I'm not crazy!*

Her mother's face swam in her vision. She saw the disappointment and the fear. "It's what's best for you. Get better, sweetheart."

Don't leave me! she screamed. *Mom!*

But her mother's face receded across the lake of blackness. She tried to swim to her, but the water came over her, pulling her down.

Hold her! Hold her!

Other voices came and spun ropes around her so she couldn't move.

God, help me!

She fought for the surface. With a great gasp, she sat up fully awake.

Her heart pounded, and she groaned. Her shaking hand came to her pounding head.

She hated that dream.

After so many years, you'd think it would stop haunting her. Honestly, it didn't happen as much as it used to. It only came now if she was overly stressed or tired.

She knew why it had visited tonight. Yesterday, her most recent column published. It didn't matter that it was October, and she hadn't heard a peep from Mr. Bells in over a month. She still felt deep anxiety, now made worse because Sheryl was getting antsy. She'd wanted Tayde to up her game and write something more sensational to get Bells to respond. Sheryl said something big was in the works and needed extra page views to push it over the edge.

While Tayde didn't specifically choose a reader letter to satisfy Sheryl's demands, she did choose one that was a little riskier. It was sure to incite debate and elicit strong emotions, which is what Sheryl wanted. Tayde hoped it didn't incite the one person she wanted to remain silent.

Tayde rolled over and looked at the time on her phone on her nightstand.

1:58

Drat! It was too early to get up for work, but she knew it would take a long while before she'd be able to go back to sleep. As usual, the nightmare had sent enough adrenaline through her veins to keep her on fight-or-flight alert for the next several hours.

She thought about getting up anyway, but Knox was asleep, and she didn't want to wake him on one of the few nights he was sleeping. Knox had been staying in more often lately, and Tayde had no idea why. She was too afraid to jinx it by asking him about it, so she tried to be silent on the subject and just appreciate that he was around more.

Not seeing another option, she rolled over and determinedly shut her eyes.

Think happy thoughts.

Her phone beeped with a notification. She immediately jerked back around and picked it up. Her eyes blinked, trying to focus on the incoming text.

```
It's me. Bells. R U up? If so, I'm ready for that
conversation.
```

Mr. Bells? Tayde hadn't received a single response after his cryptic reply to her initial email. He hadn't commented on any more of her columns. Though she still lived in enough fear to trigger nightmares, she'd kind of hoped that the mysterious Mr. Bells had dropped off the face of the earth, never to be heard from again.

Now he suddenly texted her and wanted to talk at two o'clock in the morning?

Somehow, that didn't bode well.

With shaking fingers, she quickly replied.

```
I'm up.
```

Her phone rang.

She jerked upright in bed and answered it before the first ring finished blaring.

"Hello?" she asked hesitantly, unsure if the person who answered would be a psychopath, a creep, or a run-of-the-mill insomniac.

"Hi," came the quick reply.

"So, what do I call you?" Tayde asked. With any luck, he'd confess who he was right now, and they'd be done with all the subterfuge.

There was a slight hesitation before he replied. "Bells is fine. That seems to be what everyone has dubbed me."

"You're not going to tell me your real name?"

"No, Tayde, I don't think I will."

Tayde shut her mouth and waited. He wouldn't tell her his name, yet he felt comfortable enough to call her by her first name. He also wasn't telling her why he was calling in the middle of the night. Until he started talking, he could deal with a little silence.

"Why are you up this time of night?" he finally asked.

"You called," Tayde replied simply.

"No, you were already awake. You responded to my text too quickly."

Tayde thought about lying. It was none of his business why she was awake. But then something wild shot through her, and she realized she didn't care. The room was pitch black. She hadn't bothered turning on the light, and she liked the darkness. It was like talking in a confessional box. This man was anonymous. He had no face, no name. He only existed in the world of fiction. If he wouldn't step into reality, she could tell him whatever he wanted, and it would stay a secret just like him.

She also thought she might shock him with the truth. And that sounded rather appealing.

"I have nightmares," she replied bluntly.

"You say that like it's not an out-of-the-ordinary occurrence," he observed.

Tayde was silent.

"What do you dream about?"

It was a personal question. Strangers don't ask each other to disclose the contents of their dreams. Maybe she wasn't thinking clearly. After all, it was the middle of the night. Maybe she was vulnerable with the aftereffects of her nightmare. Maybe she just didn't care. Maybe she wanted to shock this anonymous shadow who had plagued her waking hours. Maybe she needed to speak the confession she'd never breathed to another soul.

Whatever the reasons, she leaned back on the bed against

her pillows and answered the question. Really answered it.

"I dream about when I was a teenager and was so ill that the doctors and my parents decided to put me in a psychiatric hospital because they couldn't find anything physically wrong with me. Specifically, I dream about the time when I was waking up from anesthesia from a medical test. The doctor was in the room telling my mom that I had psychiatric issues and that everyone who met me could see I wasn't right. I couldn't wake up enough to say a word, but I heard every single word he said. When I did wake up, my mom took me to a psychiatric hospital, based on the doctor's recommendation. And she left me there." Her words entered the blackness around her and were absorbed almost as if they'd never existed. It was the equivalent of yelling into a black hole. Whatever she said didn't matter because it was debatable whether her words had ever existed.

"What happened?" Bells asked. There was no judgment, no sympathy. Just a request for facts, and that's what Tayde provided.

She'd never spoken to anyone, not even her parents, about what had happened next. She wouldn't have told them if they'd asked. Ghosts of memories danced through her mind, and she sorted through the pain until she fixated on the one thing that didn't hurt. "God sent someone to believe me. I arrived on the weekend, so I didn't get to see a doctor until Monday. When I finally met her, she got very angry. But not at me, at everyone else. She told them that I had a medical issue that was causing me great pain and that any depression or other issues I had were directly caused by being in constant pain. She called some of her personal doctor friends and kept me at the hospital until they figured out what was wrong."

"What was it?"

He asked the questions without emotion, and perhaps because of that, Tayde could respond without emotion.

"It was a diseased gall bladder," she said as if reporting on the weather. "I was sixteen years old. It wouldn't show up on any tests, but whenever I ate anything, I was in intense pain. Of course, I lost a bunch of weight. And, of course, people see a dangerously thin teenage girl who won't eat, and they assume anorexia. Dr. Pearson found a surgeon who believed me and diagnosed me without the classic tests and even though sixteen-year-olds supposedly don't have bad gallbladders. I had surgery to remove my gallbladder, and I was returned to my family."

"Did it work? Was that the problem?" He didn't feel sorry for her. He was simply seeking information.

Tayde never talked about her experiences to anyone and never let others in. She kept friends at an arm's distance because she had trust issues. After all, family is supposed to believe you no matter what. But she also didn't want anyone to feel sorry for her. She had overcome her past issues. Except for a few lingering nightmares, she'd left that episode of her life behind.

"I felt better in the recovery room," Tayde shared. "I've never had an issue since then. They sent my gallbladder to pathology and got scientific confirmation that it was diseased. I gained weight to a healthy level and have never had an issue since then."

"Except for the trauma."

Tayde was surprised at his insight.

"Yes. The nightmares."

"Probably not just nightmares," he said thoughtfully. "How is your relationship with your family? It's tough not to be believed by those who are supposed to love you."

Was he a shrink?

"Surprisingly good," Tayde assured honestly. "My parents felt awful, and I know they have a lot of regrets. They had a seriously ill daughter. They were afraid they would lose me. So, they did what the doctors told them. I love my parents. They aren't perfect, but I don't hold any resentment toward them."

"So, you haven't told them you still have nightmares and anxiety souvenirs."

This guy really had to be a shrink.

Tayde frowned. It was starting to feel like he was too insightful, and she wasn't sure she liked it. "No. It wouldn't change anything. No reason to tell them. The effects are minimal and don't interfere with my everyday life. Just mostly my sleep and only when I'm overly stressed."

"Why are you overly stressed tonight?"

Tayde rolled her eyes. "Because of you."

"Me?" He seemed surprised for the first time. "Do tell. I don't think I've directed a single word your way in over a month."

"But the possibility always exists," Tayde pointed out.

He paused, the silence seeming to match the darkness. Then came his quiet words. "I have nightmares too."

The statement came so softly that Tayde couldn't tell if it was serious or in jest. It was a strange experience to converse with a stranger over the phone. Tayde couldn't see his face and read his expressions. She couldn't imagine what he looked like. So much of communication was nonverbal. Eliminating everything except words made it seem like the whole experience belonged even more to a fictional world. How should she react? Did it even matter?

"But your nightmares are probably not about people carting you off to a psychiatric hospital." Tayde's attempt at a little self-deprecating humor fell flat.

"No," he said thoughtfully. "Mostly about my mom. In my dreams, I'm a teenager again. Cancer is a physical monster, and I'm standing between it and my mother, trying to protect her. I never win."

Now it was Tayde's turn to be shocked. She didn't know what to say. "I'm sorry" didn't sound enough, yet how could she convey sympathy to a nameless stranger?

Finally, she just spoke what she knew. "I hate that kind of nightmare. After so many years, you'd think they would give up and stop haunting."

"I know. Mom died a long time ago. I was barely eighteen." Still, his voice didn't carry emotion. He wasn't a robot, but he was still just speaking facts.

With sudden insight, Tayde asked, "Is that why you are awake tonight?"

"No, not tonight. I haven't gone to bed yet." He paused as if debating what to say. "I read your column."

Tayde's heart lurched into her throat, and she sat up a little straighter in bed. *This* was the reason he'd called.

"And what did you think?" she asked breathlessly.

"Your writing is always good, Tayde. It's the reason why I even bothered responding in the first place. Do you know you almost quoted a Bible verse?"

Tayde's heart beat an unsteady rhythm. Compliments for her appearance did nothing for her, but a compliment about her writing turned her to mush.

Tayde quoted, "'And let us not grow weary of doing good, for in due season we will reap, if we do not give up.' Galatians 6:9. But I couldn't quote it exactly. My boss wouldn't appreciate my bringing Christianity into a nonreligious magazine."

"But the fact that you included it and know the verse tells

me you are a Christian," he surmised.

"Yes. And the fact that you recognized the verse and asked me the question makes me wonder if—"

"Yes, I'm a believer." His voice was strong and certain.

Tayde felt another thrill. He liked her writing, *and* he was a believer!

"I've been up thinking about a response to your column this week."

And all the magical butterflies fell to the ground.

Why? If it was good, why did he need to bother responding?

She took a slow, shallow breath before venturing casually, "Do you want to talk about what you're thinking?"

"Well, I kinda already wrote it. That's why I'm up so late."

"Okay. Do you want to email it to me? I can look it over, and we can discuss it." She reached down beside her bed and fumbled for her laptop in the dark.

"Well, I kinda already posted it."

Tayde's heart stopped. She sat up stiffly in bed.

"You posted it," she echoed numbly.

"Yeah, just a little bit ago. I just wanted to give you a heads-up."

Shock and anger vied for top billing. "So, you called me to give me a 'heads-up' that you wrote and posted another letter to humiliate me?"

"It doesn't humiliate you, Tayde," he disagreed quietly. "I've never done that. And you told me to call."

"I meant *before* you posted! Not *after*!" she objected. "But there's no way. You couldn't have found the woman mentioned in the letter. And why would you want to?"

"Just read the letter, Tayde."

She hated his calm tone, especially when she was the opposite of calm. "Why do you hate me so? What have I ever done to you?"

"I don't hate you, Tayde. I just—"

"I have to go. Thanks for the wide-awake nightmare, Mr. Bells." She ended the call with a shaking finger.

She was so angry. She'd confessed all that personal stuff—things she'd never breathed a word of to anyone else. And the whole time, he knew he'd already thrown her under the bus.

That was the one and only conversation she'd ever have with that man. She'd never speak to him again.

Choking down tears, she logged onto her computer and brought up the column published yesterday. There were already lots of comments, but it was the middle of the night. Sheryl wouldn't have had a chance to put on all the bells and whistles for *the* comment.

It wasn't difficult to find. His was the really long one. With a deep breath, she started reading.

Dear Ms. Wright,

Let me introduce you to the woman mentioned in Do-Gooder's letter. She dropped out of high school at the age of sixteen because she got pregnant. She married her boyfriend. He then proceeded to abuse her. He finally left her when she was pregnant with their second child. She has difficulty holding a job because of her lack of education and the learning challenges that made school difficult to begin with.

She finally found a man who works a steady job and treats her well. At least he doesn't abuse her or the children. They've had some difficulties and lost their low-income apartment due to a misunderstanding. They now live in an RV, waiting for more low-income housing to open up. She's applied for local jobs and is waiting to hear back, but any job she has must be within walking distance. Her boyfriend needs the car to get to work.

It embarrassed her to ask for help on social media. She is not bringing in any money, so she has no control over what her boyfriend spends his money on, including cigarettes. There was not enough money left to buy food, and she couldn't stand for her children to go hungry.

You didn't know that she was there when Do-Gooder brought the groceries. She was hiding in the RV, too humiliated to accept the groceries herself.

Full confession: I do not know the woman mentioned above. Maybe the fictionalized scenario is true. Maybe it isn't. The point is that we don't know someone's personal story. We can't read thoughts and feelings. We can't know what others are going through or why they react in certain ways.

But there are a few things we can know.

Most people are doing the best they can, given their current circumstances. Most people don't wake up intending to make bad decisions or hurt others that day. That doesn't make their sins blameless or their bad choices excusable. But it does mean we should believe the best of people and be generous with our compassion and stingy with our judgment.

Food for children should always be prioritized over cigarettes. But we don't know the circumstances that created that unfortunate moment. I'm not advocating for her choices or her lifestyle. I'm not saying she is right or shouldn't bear responsibility. I'm saying that everyone could use a little empathy and compassion. I do not believe someone needs to be worthy of generosity or grace to receive it. There are instances in my own life where I received both, even though I didn't deserve them.

Maybe Do-Gooder was taken advantage of. I don't know the actual truth of the situation. But I'd rather be taken advantage of than ignore a legitimate need. What is the greater wrong? That you feel taken advantage of, or that children go hungry? If it means children have food for lunch, you can take advantage of me repeatedly, and I'd count that a good deal.

Do-Gooder should hold her head high that she did such a beautiful, generous act for someone who may not have deserved it. The cigarettes, the dogs... those are just noise. The truth is that children got to eat lunch that day because of her. And that is a whole lot of right.

Can you hear the bells?

Tayde finished reading, shut her laptop, and set it aside. Then she laid her head back on the pillow and turned toward the window. Tears streamed down her face as she sobbed silently.

He'd done a good job. The content of the letter didn't upset her. How could it? It was a beautifully written letter. What upset her most was that he was right. He'd one-upped her again, saying all the beautiful things she should have thought to say and didn't. Once again, she'd misjudged someone, and it was on display for the whole world to see.

She would have cried herself to sleep, except she didn't sleep.

Chapter Ten

Tayde irritably tossed the dish into the sink. The resulting clamor echoed a little louder than she intended.

Knox came up beside her. "I guess breaking the dishes is one method of dealing with them. But rather expensive. Move over. You have every dish in the apartment shaking in fear."

Tayde sighed, lifted her hands in surrender, and backed away from the sink for her brother to take her place.

It was sweet of him to take over. He did the dishes just as much as she did. If they were keeping score, it was probably her turn. But Knox was right. She wasn't exactly in a condition to guarantee the well-being of any inanimate object right now.

"Why such a rotten mood?" Knox asked, taking over the sponge and starting to scrub.

"Nothing new," she grumbled. "Just Mr. Bells' drama."

"But you haven't heard from him in weeks, right? Not since

the post about the woman who needed food for her kids. It's the beginning of December. When was that?"

"Late October," Tayde admitted. "But it's like a cloud hanging over me. He made me look like a horrible human for thinking badly of a woman trying to feed her children. Sheryl keeps putting pressure on me to cover more hot-button issues, and I never know when Mr. Bells will hit me with another zinger."

"You have his phone number, right? Couldn't you just call and ask him for his scheduled efforts at ruining your life?"

Leave it to Knox to devise a practical and thoroughly impossible solution!

"I can't contact him!" Tayde objected as if he'd just suggested she fly to the moon.

"Why not?" he asked, acting as if he'd just managed to use a paperclip to straighten the Leaning Tower of Pisa. "You did it before."

"Yes, but I wasn't supposed to," Tayde pointed out in exasperation. "And see what it got me? I haven't emailed, texted, or talked to him since that single night when he called me."

"You won't contact him because you're still mad."

Why did Knox insist on reducing complex issues to kindergarten simplicity? Now Tayde felt compelled to defend her actions. "He could have told me that he'd posted a letter immediately. But he didn't. He got me talking and sharing about personal stuff. Then he stabbed me in the back."

Somehow, none of that sounded as good out loud as it did in her head.

"Oh, I get it. He got you to open up." Knox turned his head away from the sink and winked at her. "You liked him."

"He's a jerk," Tayde bit back.

"The guy who wrote those letters is not a jerk," Knox insisted, steadily rinsing the dishes and positioning them in the dishwasher. "Mr. Bells is the unofficial 'most eligible bachelor' of Brighton Falls. Every unattached woman in half the country dreams of the smart, understanding Mr. Bells who writes like a poet and is the Robin Hood of kindness."

"That's ridiculous," Tayde scoffed. She reached over and grabbed a hand towel, ready to help dry any dishes that needed hand washing. "Nobody even knows for sure he's mister."

Knox cocked a grin her way. "You do."

"He might be married," she shot back, refusing to give him even an inch.

Knox rolled his eyes and then turned a longsuffering look her way. "He called you in the middle of the night. He's not married. Come on, Tayde, just text him. You've been making yourself miserable for weeks. It's like you're obsessed but unwilling to do anything about it. Now you're in a foul mood for no good reason."

"I have another column due, and I have no idea what to write," Tayde confessed. "Sheryl switched my schedule because of Christmas. She wants an extra column published before, instead of after, Christmas. I have a column that's supposed to be published tomorrow morning, and I have no idea what to write. Every letter I read, I think of how he'll roast whatever response I make. It's like I'm paralyzed and too afraid to look like a fool again."

A knock sounded at the door. Knox dried his hands and walked over to open it while Tayde stood moodily with her arms crossed over her front. Knox opened the door, letting Frankie enter with a plate full of Christmas cookies in her hands.

"What's wrong with Tayde?" she asked as she passed to put

the plate on the counter.

Frankie had made a habit of showing up on random nights, usually with a plate of homemade goodies for Knox to enjoy. Tayde enjoyed it when Frankie showed up and suspected Knox did too. They'd often play card games or watch a movie, and Tayde wondered if Knox had started staying closer to home because of the possibility that Frankie might show up. Of course, he seemed clueless and never treated Frankie as more than a friend. Tayde stayed out of it. She knew better than to hope for something more than friendship between the two.

"She's mooning over Mr. Bells again," Knox reported. "Got writer's block because she's too afraid of what he'll think."

"If I just knew who he was, I'd be okay," Tayde insisted. "But he's like a phantom, and my imagination can't take it. I'd feel more comfortable with my own if he were a real, flesh-and-blood person with faults and quirks."

Knox cocked his head thoughtfully. "That's a profound way of looking at it. Here I thought you were just mad."

"Then find him," Frankie said easily. "Unmask Mr. Bells."

Great, now Tayde had another person convinced he or she could solve the world's problems with a paper clip. "How do you propose I do that?" Tayde asked tartly.

Frankie grabbed one of her own sugar cookies and started munching. "You talked to him. He must have given you some clues. You know for sure he was a guy. How old did he sound?"

Tayde reluctantly considered the question. "About my age," she confessed.

Happy with a small bit of success, Frankie tried again. "What other personal details did he tell you?"

Needing fuel for thought, Tayde couldn't resist and grabbed a cookie for herself. Her mind drifted back to that late-night conversation from over a month ago, but she came up blank.

"He didn't really say anything about himself. We mostly talked about me."

Frankie pointed at Tayde with her cookie in hand. "Tayde, you need to find this guy and marry him. A man who is willing to talk about you more than himself is the equivalent of a unicorn."

"Hey!" Knox protested, but the word sounded more like a grunt since his mouth was full of cookie.

Frankie smiled at Knox sweetly. "I never said you weren't a unicorn, Knox."

"He did tell me his mother passed away from cancer when he was eighteen," Tayde said, trying to recall anything useful from their conversation.

"Well, I'm not sure we can google that. But detectives get by with less." Frankie tilted her head back and looked upward in a thoughtful pose.

Silence stretched as all three of them reached for another cookie and searched for clues that probably didn't exist.

Finally, Frankie spoke. "In all the crime shows, the detectives always go back to the first crime someone committed because they assume that was the personal trigger for the crime."

"Like a serial killer?" Tayde protested. "Frankie, that's ridiculous! He's not a criminal."

"No, but the same logic might work," Frankie insisted. "He's been on a kindness spree. But maybe he knew the first victim."

Wide-eyed, Tayde shook her head in protest. "What victim? There wasn't a victim!"

"Your first victim, Tayde," Frankie clarified. "Maybe he knows the Paulsens."

Tayde put her cookie on a napkin on the counter. She'd suddenly lost her appetite. "Now I'm the criminal?"

"She has a point," Knox mused, finally taking a break from

his cookie consumption long enough to participate in the conversation. "His letter sounded like he knew the Paulsens personally. If his friends were hurt by your column, he would have a motive to defend them. Didn't you tell me the second letter was in response to someone asking for his help? By the time he sent two letters, he was kind of in too deep, and everyone was expecting and wanting him to respond again. But Frankie is right. The Fourth of July was the instigating event."

"Did you find out any information about the Paulsens?" Frankie asked.

Tayde shook her head. "No. I read Tori Paulsen's obituary, but that's as far as I went. I felt so bad about the whole thing, and finding out more about them only made me feel worse."

"If you want to find Mr. Bells, you'll have to give the Paulsens a closer look," Frankie said firmly.

Tayde wasn't sure she could do that. She felt nauseated at the thought of meeting them and asking them questions in an undercover effort to find their friend. Hadn't she already bothered them enough? She didn't want to hurt them more.

"Or you could just ask the guy," Knox said simply. "Skip the detective work. Skip the clues. Just ask Mr. Bells your questions directly. You have his number."

And Knox was back with his paperclip solution.

"He won't answer," Tayde said, impatiently brushing off the suggestion yet again.

"How do you know?" Knox pressed.

"Because I know," Tayde said. Even as she said it, she realized how childish she sounded. "I already tried. He wouldn't tell me his name."

Knox shrugged. "So, ask a different question."

Finally fed up, Tayde turned to him with her eyes flashing and her hands impatiently perched on her hips. "You want me to text him and ask him what exactly?"

Knox threw his hands up. "Anything! Seems a whole lot easier than tracking down his friends. He won't tell you his name, but maybe he'll answer something else."

Tayde shook her head, giving up on the conversation. "You're ridiculous. You know I'm not going to contact him."

"Sheesh, Tayde! I'm done. I can't handle you moping around here anymore." He reached over Tayde's shoulder and snatched her phone off the counter. "If you won't text him, I will."

"Knox, you wouldn't!" Tayde took off after him, but he danced out of the way.

She got close and made a swipe, but he leaped onto the couch and tiptoed across it, always keeping the phone out of Tayde's reach.

Tayde suddenly stopped and folded her arms over her chest. "You can't get into my phone anyway. It's password protected."

Knox's fingers tapped over the screen. "Let's see... there he is. You labeled him in your contacts as Mr. Bell."

Tayde lunged at him. "You know my password?"

Knox laughed and dodged away.

Frankie offered her hand out for the phone, but Knox danced away from her, too, proclaiming, "Sorry, Frankie, I can't trust you. This job needs done, and I'm the one to do it."

Tayde made another swipe, coming up with only a fleeting handful of his shirt. Laughing, he sprinted away, jumped over the back of the couch, and skidded into the bathroom.

Tayde distinctly heard the sound of the lock engaging. Tayde banged on the door with her fist. "Knox, please! I don't want to text him."

"It's time to swallow your pride," he called through the door. "I'm here to help you choke it down. Don't worry. I'll keep it simple. How about... 'Can I ask you a question?' There, the message is sent."

"You... You..." Tayde wanted to call him a name. A really bad one that her mother wouldn't approve of. But she was so flabbergasted that her wide vocabulary was reduced to zero.

The bathroom door opened. Knox calmly handed her phone back. "There you go. All yours."

Tayde glanced down at the screen, seeing that Mr. Bells had already responded to the question posed by Knox. As she watched, more words appeared on the screen.

```
Ask away.
You get 1 question.
And I reserve the right to pass and request a
different question.
```

"One question," Tayde breathed. "He'll answer one question."

Her attention diverted by the result, Tayde immediately forgave Knox his transgression and forgot she'd been screaming at him twenty seconds ago.

Frankie hurried over to peer down at Tayde's phone screen. "It's gotta be a good one," she pointed out. "What's his job? Where does he work? What's his address? Date of birth and social security number?"

"He'll just pass on all of those," Tayde dismissed. "Maybe I should stick with a yes or no question."

"You've got to start somewhere," Frankie encouraged.

Tayde bit her lip in thought. She wanted to know what he did for a living. She wondered if he was a writer for another magazine or a newspaper. Maybe he was even someone she knew or worked with. As Frankie had said, Mr. Bells consistently "wrote her pants off," and those writing skills were not average.

He wouldn't answer what he did for a living, but maybe if she came about it sideways, she could get the answer anyway. She needed to start somewhere. She fully expected him to pass on multiple questions before finding one insignificant enough to respond to.

Before she lost her nerve, she typed.

```
Were you an English major in college?
```

The reply came swiftly.

```
Yes.
```

That was it? That was what she wasted her one question on?

"That wasn't really helpful," she moaned, handing the traitorous phone to Frankie. "I thought he'd pass on a few dozen before answering one. Now all I know is that he majored in English. That's not something I can google either."

Frankie glanced at the screen and tossed the phone to the couch. "Well, I'm out of here. I'll leave you to your mystery. I've got nothing left."

"Thanks for the cookies, Frankie," Knox called, grabbing another as he passed by on his way to the couch.

Frankie made her exit. As soon as the door shut, Knox turned to Tayde with his mouth half-full of cookie. "You know, one option is to have a conversation with the guy and see if anything comes up."

Tayde groaned. It was the same suggestion he'd made at least two other times. He always made it sound so easy, as if he thought no one else in the world had thought of this ridiculously simple, foolproof solution.

"Why do you even care?" Tayde asked irritably. Why couldn't he just leave her alone?

Knox frowned up at her from where he sprawled on the couch. "Because I'm tired of you moping around so focused on yourself all the time. So what if you were embarrassed? Get over it. Other people exist."

Knox just didn't get it. It wasn't that she was embarrassed once and just couldn't let it go. It wasn't a one-time incident. It was continual. Everywhere she went, she was grilled with questions and openly shamed for the columns she'd written. People saw Bells as the hero who put the villain in her place. And Tayde was apparently the villain.

Now Knox was criticizing her, just like everyone else. Her immediate reaction was anger.

Without thinking it through, she snapped back, "And if you didn't spend your time focused on yourself, you'd be able to see that what you're looking for is right in front of you!"

Knox's face scrunched in confusion. "What are you talking about? What's right in front of me?"

"Exactly," Tayde shot back with more than a little superiority in her tone.

Knox jumped up from the couch. "You know what, Tayde? You're not the only one who has bad days. I think you need to take a few more lessons from Mr. Bells."

Knox stomped off to his room and slammed the door shut.

Tayde sank down on the couch and leaned her head back, instant regret washing over her. Knox was right. She'd been so focused on her own troubles that she hadn't noticed anyone else.

She stood, pushed aside her work and worries, and dragged herself over to Knox's door. She knocked lightly. "Hey, Knox. I'm sorry. You're right. I've been clueless lately. Can I come in?"

Tayde didn't hear a response, but the knob turned under

her grasp. She pushed it open to find Knox spread out on his bed, watching her with arms folded moodily across his front.

She stepped into the room and perched at the end of his bed, exactly as she'd done many times growing up. They'd always had a close relationship. Knox could always talk to her. Occasionally, it occurred to Tayde that it wasn't a two-way street. She didn't confide in Knox the way he confided in her, but she was fine with that. She was the older sister. In some ways, Mom was right. Tayde was the strong, stable one. But she'd been so upset she hadn't kept up on her end of their usual relationship.

"So, what's going on?" she asked. "Why was today a bad day?"

Knox laced his hands behind his head and leaned back against his pillow, not looking at her. "Usual stuff at work. It just means tomorrow will be a rotten day too."

Knox usually enjoyed his job as a junior high science teacher. He'd always loved science and was still a big kid in many ways. He got along great with his students and was a favorite teacher at his school. He was the perfect combination of academics and fun. Most days, he came home in a good mood.

"What happened?" Tayde pushed. He wanted to talk. He just needed a little coaxing to get there.

Finally, he confessed, "In one of my classes, a student with known anger issues got mad and threw a chair. It missed another student's face by less than two inches. I followed protocol and got the student out of the classroom. He calmed down and spent the rest of the period with behavioral support and didn't return to class. No one was hurt, but it shook the students up pretty bad. I'm sure I'll have to deal with lots of irate parents tomorrow. I can't blame them. Someone could have been hurt."

"If the student has known anger issues and is a danger to other students, why is he in class?" Tayde asked, voicing the obvious question.

Knox's mouth formed a thin line. "That's the exact question I will have to answer over and over tomorrow."

"What will you say?" Tayde asked curiously. What could a teacher say in that kind of incident?

Knox waved his hand and replied stiffly, "Standard stuff. Every child is entitled to an education. No one was hurt. Everyone followed protocol."

Tayde shifted to problem-solving mode. "If he needs to be in class, can't they get him his own assistant?"

"There's no money for that, Tayde," Knox said, his tone colored with sad amusement.

Tayde shook her head, finding that answer inadequate. "But how can you teach effectively if there's always a danger that a student might blow up and hurt other students?"

Knox cocked his head. "And that is a question I cannot answer."

Tayde's brow furrowed. "I'm sorry, Knox. That sounds like a no-win scenario. The student is required to be in class, but you are not provided the necessary tools to keep the other students safe. I don't know the solution, but I do know it isn't right."

Tayde's eyes lit up. "Wait... right. That's it! Knox, I need to write about you for my column!"

Knox sat up in the bed, instant panic stripping his face of color. "What? No... Absolutely not, Tayde. There are privacy issues. I could get in a huge amount of hot water. Maybe even lose my job."

"I'm not an idiot," Tayde chided, shooting a glance his way before pacing the floor as she outlined her plans out loud. "We wouldn't use real names or anything. But this is probably an issue schools, teachers, students, and parents around the country are trying to deal with. What you experienced today is scary, and we shouldn't wait around until something worse happens to do something. Where's a pencil and paper? I need to write that line down before I forget."

Knox stood and folded his arms across his front as he faced his sister. "I can't write a letter to your magazine. You know that all of the writing genes fell in your lap. I won't do it."

"Then I'll do it for you," Tayde said easily. "Don't worry. I won't use any names or anything that could identify you or the school. I'll even let you read it before I send it to Sheryl."

"So, you plan to write a letter yourself, as if someone else wrote it. Then you're going to respond to the letter yourself. Isn't that unethical or illegal or something? I don't think the same person can write both letters. It's dishonest or something."

"There's no rule that says I can't," Tayde said brightly. "The first one won't really be my letter. It's your letter. I'm just writing it on your behalf. Nobody but you and me will ever know."

"Tayde, that's insane."

"No. It's genius." Tayde didn't wait for any more of Knox's objections. She hurried back into the living room and grabbed her laptop.

This was it. This time, she'd write a fantastic column that truly made a difference and turned wrongs to right. This column could even help Knox! It had everything. Kids, education, safety—lots of potential emotions to please Sheryl. And there was nothing for which Mr. Bells could add his two cents. What was he going to say—that kids weren't entitled to be safe?

She'd be nice, of course. She wouldn't say anything inflammatory. But right was right. There was no other side when it came to child safety, education, and giving teachers the tools they needed to teach. And she had the inside scoop. No matter what fantastic tale of fiction he tried to weave, she could refute it. This time, she personally knew the writer of the reader's letter. Well, she would ghostwrite the reader's letter, but she knew the person who owned the experience.

This time, she fully intended to silence Mr. Bells.

Dear Ms. Wright,

I am a junior high teacher. I am writing this letter to raise awareness of one of the issues many teachers, students, and schools face today. How do we balance students' educational rights and needs with their safety?

It seems obvious that children should be safe to attend school and learn. But the reality is more complicated.

I have a student in class who has known anger issues. Recently, he got upset and threw a chair. It missed another student's face by less than two inches. No one was hurt, but someone could have been. Let me assure readers that everyone followed proper procedures and the student received the appropriate behavior management support outlined in our protocols. But it left the students (and me) shaken up. What if the chair had been two inches closer? What if a student had been hurt?

Legally, every student is entitled to a free public education. But what do we do in a scenario where a student's right to education interferes with other students' safety?

This student is only one of many with significant behavioral challenges. Funding does not exist for us to hire a personal aide for every student with behavioral issues. If there is a solution, it's likely a complicated one. Obviously, if the solution were simple, there would be nothing to discuss. I just wanted people to be aware of the issue

If you come across any teachers in your daily walk today, tell them you appreciate them. They are trying to provide students with education while keeping them safe under circumstances that sometimes seem hopeless.

I don't know what the answers are. But I know the problem, and I keep circling back to the idea that children should be provided a safe environment in which to learn. How to make that happen—I have no idea.

*Sincerely,
A teacher*

Dear Hero Teacher,

Thank you for being a teacher. Thank you for being a hero. Not only do you teach our children, but you also care about them. You want better for them, even if you don't know what better looks like.

As you said, children have the right to education, but they also should be safe while receiving that education. Further, teachers should be safe while teaching and not have to worry about the safety of their students or themselves.

If a student has known anger issues that present a threat to other students, why is he or she in class? If that chair had impacted another student's head or face, it could have resulted in long-term damage or even been fatal. If protocol was being followed and yet this incident still happened, the protocol should be changed so it never happens again. How can teachers teach effectively if they are concerned about safety? How can students learn effectively if, at any moment, a chair could be flung at their heads?

Like you, I don't have the answers. But this is an issue that shouldn't be ignored. What you and your students experienced is scary, and we shouldn't wait until something worse happens before doing something. Maybe the solution involves trained child psychology specialists, more staff, better protocols, offering alternative education, or a myriad of other possibilities. The student with anger issues also deserves to have his needs met. If he is acting out, that tells us the system isn't working for him, either.

A person's rights end where another person's begins. And if student education is detrimentally impacted because of another student, then we can't simply carry on with business as usual, especially when the impact involves safety.

Let me encourage students, parents, teachers, administrators, school districts, and lawmakers to think outside the box. Safety is not too much to ask for both our heroes of today and our heroes of tomorrow.

Sincerely,
T. Wright

Isaiah

Isaiah sat down in his usual chair at the back table of the Science lab and waited for the bell to signal the start of class. Science was his favorite. The only thing he didn't like about it was that sometimes other students behaved badly. Mr. Wright was pretty good about keeping control of the class, but sometimes, it was hard to wait to get to the fun stuff because other kids weren't behaving. That's why he liked sitting at the back table. Several of his other friends sat with him, and they did a pretty good job of tuning out the noise to get their work done.

A loud clanging made him jump. He jerked around to see a chair clatter to the floor. Zach hurriedly backed away from the fallen chair and took a seat at the back table beside Isaiah. Though he'd knocked the chair over, the startled look on his face clearly said he hadn't intended to.

Isaiah knew Zach had some issues, but he liked him. He was smart and usually chose to sit with Isaiah and his friends in class. While it was known that he had anger issues, at least he wasn't obnoxious like some of the other students.

"Hey, Zach," a girl named Alicia called loudly. "Pick up the chair. You knocked it over. Pick it up."

"No," Zach said simply.

"You've got to pick it up," Alicia insisted. "You knocked it over."

It wasn't even Alicia's chair. Isaiah had no idea why she was insisting Zach pick it up.

"Yeah," another girl insisted. "Pick it up, Zach. Pick it up."

"You're such a loser, Zach. If you knock it down, you gotta pick it up."

"Look at him. He's just sitting there."

The razzing came fast and unrelenting.

Isaiah stood, walked over, and righted the chair.

"Why did you do that?" one of the girls asked. "It was his job."

"I'm going to tell the teacher," another girl called, her voice shrill. "He should have picked it up."

Isaiah had just sat back down when a pencil flew by him. He looked up to see an angry expression on Zach's face, and his fingers poised as if he'd just let the pencil fly.

A string of curse words filled the air.

"Hey! He just threw a pencil!" Alicia yelped.

"You can't do that!" Another girl protested.

"You'll hurt someone! Don't you know not to throw things?"

"What are you? Three years old? Sheesh! He threw a pencil

at me!"

Isaiah looked around for Mr. Wright, but he was outside in the hall monitoring the activity between classes.

They needed to stop. Why couldn't they just stop? He looked at his friends, but none of them made eye contact with him. Nobody knew what to do.

"Maybe you should go back to kindergarten, Zach. You need to learn the rules."

"He almost hit me. I could sue you!"

Please stop! Just leave him alone!

But the abuse continued, the words flying at Zach, needling, pinching, aggravating in unceasing torment. Isaiah wished he knew what to do. They'd just turn their abuse on him if he told them to stop. They were like a pack of wolves circling, each taking their turn nipping at their prey.

Isaiah looked down, studying the fake wood grain design on the table, wishing he were anywhere but here.

Suddenly, a guttural yell slashed through the room. Isaiah looked up right as a massive object sailed right by his head. He felt the movement of the air as it passed in a whisper before his face, followed immediately by a thunderous crash that sent vibrations through the whole classroom.

Shocked silence filled the void left when the impact chased the air from the room.

Isaiah's gaze went from the upturned chair smashed against the wall back to where Zach stood, red-faced and breathing heavily, his now empty hands at his sides.

Mr. Wright was suddenly there, coaxing Zach out of the room.

Isaiah's brain struggled to catch up with what had just happened and what was happening now. The group of girls began twittering. As he left, Zach looked back at them, his eyes glaring and flashing angrily.

Mr. Wright soon returned. "Is everyone okay?" he asked.

"It almost hit Isaiah in the head," someone supplied.

"Isaiah, you ok?" Mr. Wright asked, spearing him with a direct, assessing gaze.

Isaiah nodded and did his best to hide his shaking hands. "Fine." The memory of the chair brushing past him replayed through his mind, and he shivered.

"Ok, guys. We need to do our best to ignore Zach and not do anything to agitate him."

"We weren't," Alicia volunteered. "He just threw the chair for no reason. I could have been killed!"

"Thankfully, nobody was hurt," Mr. Wright said soothingly. "I'm sorry that happened, but Zach's going to calm down and be fine. Let's get started on the lesson for today."

The rest of the class passed uneventfully, as did the rest of the day. But Isaiah was still bothered that evening. He thought about telling his parents but worried it would only worsen the situation. If they knew what had happened, they'd probably be upset he was almost hurt. They'd blame Zach, just like the school. Zach might get in even more trouble if they contacted Mr. Wright or the school.

Isaiah finished his homework and readied for bed, never breathing a word to anyone about what had happened. He didn't feel guilt; there was nothing to feel guilty about. He felt sorrow. He hated the way Zach had been treated. His reaction was wrong, but the actions that incited his reaction were also wrong. Since Isaiah had sat there and watched it happen, he hadn't been able to shake the sense of helplessness.

The next morning, he woke feeling no better. He dreaded school, and with sudden clarity, he realized why. He was afraid of a repeat performance. Nothing could stop the girls from doing the same thing to Zach today. After all, according to everyone else, it was Zach's fault.

The thought was too much for Isaiah. He couldn't go through that experience again. He couldn't sit and do nothing. He couldn't let it happen to Zach again, and he couldn't risk someone getting hurt if Zach lost control.

He got ready for school quickly and asked his mom to drop him off a little early. She was satisfied with his explanation that he needed to talk to a teacher and didn't ask for more specifics. Isaiah was nervous, but he went directly to Mr. Wright's classroom. The fears clamored in his mind, begging for his attention.

What if I can't explain it well? What if it's still Zach's fault? What if the others find out I told? What if it doesn't help, and it happens all over again anyway? What if Mr. Wright thinks bad of me?

He gritted his teeth, pushed all the thoughts aside, and walked into the classroom. "Mr. Wright," he called. His voice cracked.

Mr. Wright looked up from his computer and stood to meet him.

Isaiah cleared his throat and tried again. "Mr. Wright, can I talk to you about what happened yesterday?"

Chapter Twelve

Tayde

Tayde laid the dress out on her bed, spreading the full skirt out for maximum effect. She was excited. She felt like the stress of the past few months had finally resolved into a happy ending, and she allowed herself to feel the anticipation of tonight's events.

It was safe to relax and enjoy tonight. At least, that's what she told herself. Her latest column came out Friday of last week. She'd had so many positive comments from people agreeing with her and thanking her for spotlighting such important issues facing the world of education today. It was now Saturday. It had been over a full week, and Mr. Bells had not made an appearance. She'd even posted another column.

Though the new one wasn't nearly such a hot-button topic, it had also met with silence so far. Mr. Bells' previous comments had been posted long before now, and Tayde felt entirely safe and justified in feeling intense relief mixed with a tiny bit of victory.

She'd won. She'd written a hot-button column, and Mr. Bells had nothing to say about it. She'd drawn attention to an important issue and not felt wrong in doing so. Even Sheryl was pleased. Maybe not as pleased as she would have been if Bells had responded, but she was satisfied enough that Tayde hadn't faced another summons to her cat lair office.

The magazine was holding its employee Christmas party at the annual gala sponsored by a local investment company. Though the official announcement would come tonight, Sheryl had dropped enough hints that Tayde was fairly certain the important news would include the investment company's purchase of a certain newly redesigned magazine. Tayde was convinced that a wealthy new benefactor would mean the magazine would be poised for launching to a larger audience. Though several of her posts had gained national attention, more funding would enable greater consistent visibility. The thought both excited and terrified her. She'd always dreamed of being a respected writer with a national reach. Though it wasn't exactly what she'd dreamed, the reality felt so close.

Tayde picked up the small mask that matched her dress and examined it carefully, ensuring the glue held. The party tonight was a masquerade ball. The organizers had felt it very clever to make the gala adhere to all safety recommendations but do it in a fun way. Instead of requiring all participants to wear medical masks, they were allowing any mask, provided they covered the mouth and nose. With the danger of the pandemic past, the whole idea seemed more artsy than necessary, but everyone had embraced the idea of a funky masquerade ball, putting a lot of effort into their masks and attire.

Tayde looked at her mask critically. From one angle, the mask adorned with feathers and pearls looked beautiful, especially when paired with her matching gown and faux fur stole jacket. However, from another angle, Tayde thought the mask looked cheap and worried it might appear like an unfortunate bird had chosen her face as its final resting place.

With a frown, she tugged slightly at one of the feathers. A beep from her phone stilled her movements, rescuing the mask from her attention.

```
Mr. Bells: I liked your column.
```

Tayde's stomach leaped into her throat. She hadn't heard from Mr. Bells since Knox had texted him on her behalf, and he'd responded. Tayde had never bothered replying to his one-word admittance that he had majored in English. She hadn't purposely been rude, but she was worried that further communication would encourage him to respond to another column. So, she'd been silent. And he'd been silent.

Until now.

If he hadn't responded to her column and now said he liked it, was that it? Or was there some hidden agenda? Was this truly a compliment?

She didn't know how to respond and didn't want to encourage further discussion for him to relate all the points of the column he disagreed with. Finally, she typed out two simple words.

```
Tayde: Thank you.
```

She bit her lip in anxiety as she watched the three little dots indicating that he was typing.

```
Mr. Bells: I especially liked the part where you
said, "The student with anger issues also deserves
to have his needs met."
```

A delighted smile lifted the corners of her mouth. It really was a compliment!

```
Tayde: I thought you'd like that. I've learned that
it's good to think of both sides.
```

She felt successful. Mr. Bells hadn't commented because she'd done it all on her own. She'd written a balanced piece that he couldn't find fault with. The three dots disappeared into another text.

```
Mr. Bells: Getting ready for the party tonight?
```

Tayde plopped down beside her dress in shock. How did he know about the party? Suddenly creeped out, she looked to the curtained window and checked every shadow in the room, wondering if he somehow watched her. Finding nothing amiss, she skipped the subtlety and typed out the obvious question.

```
Tayde: How do you know about the party?

Mr. Bells: Getting my tux ready.
```

Her heart leaped painfully. He was going to the party? How? Why? Maybe Mr. Bells really was another magazine employee! But as soon as the thought materialized, she dismissed it. The gala wasn't simply for the magazine. It was an annual event open to the community. A large portion of the ticket sales went to charities, and many wealthy citizens and businesses participated. With the gala sold out every year, tickets were a commodity. The employees at Chronicle were especially thrilled about being guests at the event. Tayde had never attended before, but that excitement paled compared to the burst of adrenaline at the thought that Mr. Bells might also attend.

Wanting no doubt as to his meaning, Tayde asked the question directly.

```
Tayde: Will you be at the gala?

Mr. Bells: I'll be there with bells on.
```

Tayde's breath caught. She was finally going to meet Mr. Bells. What would she do? What would she say? Her hand shook so badly that she had to delete several versions with typos before she managed to get the question right.

```
Tayde: How will I know you?
```

Tayde held her breath and waited. But the three dots never blinked. Eventually, she had to breathe again. That's it? He was going to quip that ridiculous pun about being there with bells on and leave it at that?

Spotting the time, she tossed her phone down on the bed. Now she'd need to rush to get ready. She'd hoped to have a fun, relaxing evening, but she wasn't even at the party yet, and her nerves were shot. How could she enjoy any of it if she was constantly looking over her shoulder and wondering at the secret identity of every man in the room?

She put on her dress and rushed through her hair and makeup. She'd arranged to meet Frankie outside the building downtown, and she didn't want her friend waiting for her in the cold. They'd had the option of bringing a date but had opted not to. Tayde wanted to arrange for Knox to be Frankie's date, but Knox was busy with a science club event tonight. It was probably for the best that it hadn't worked out. Knox had been acting weird lately and would've been lousy company. For once, he wouldn't spill his guts to Tayde, and Tayde hadn't found time to corner him on his anxious moping. She made a mental note to buy some ice cream tomorrow and use large quantities of it in a targeted attempt to drag his troubles out of him.

Tayde was out the door in record time and made it downtown to the parking garage just a few minutes later than she'd wanted. She met Frankie at the door as planned. At the sight of her friend, Tayde wished Knox's science club event had been on another night. Frankie looked wonderful. Her purple dress was stylish and fit her well. She'd taken extra effort with her hair and makeup. Maybe if Knox saw her looking like this, he'd move her out of the friend category and into the love-of-his-life category.

"You clean up well," Tayde told her as they walked through the front doors.

"That's not exactly encouraging, Tayde," Frankie said dryly. "I'm wearing a mask. So, everything but my face cleans up well?"

Tayde laughed. "No, your everything cleans up well. And the mask looks good too." Frankie's green mask matched her dress. The purple and green sparkles gave it a Mardi Gras vibe, and the colors drew attention to the beautiful green eyes behind her glasses.

"Maybe," Frankie muttered doubtfully. "But I turn into a pumpkin at midnight."

"Good to know. But I wish Knox could see you before that." She raised a teasing eyebrow in Frankie's direction and watched her reaction.

A soft blush crept up her neck. "Knox doesn't like pumpkins."

"Not true," Tayde shot back. "Pumpkin pie is his favorite, remember?"

Once admitted to the festivities, Tayde and Frankie walked around to see the beautifully decorated trees lining the perimeter of the ballroom floor. Each tree was unique. Tayde could have spent ten minutes on each tree, admiring the intricate details of the ornaments' décor. She couldn't decide which her favorite was, but she liked the one decorated with angels. She also liked the rustic one decorated entirely with items from nature, including hand-carved ornaments. But just when she thought she'd narrowed it down to two, she caught sight of the retro aluminum tree redesigned to include a LED light display and funky vintage ornaments.

"Ooh," she breathed. "That's awesome."

"You're so weird," Frankie laughed. "You are a bizarre mixture of completely opposing tastes."

"Just means I'm well-balanced," Tayde offered.

"No. I don't think that's what it means," Frankie said with an ornery grin.

Tayde turned and looked over the ballroom, scanning the face of every man she could see.

"Who are you looking for?" Frankie asked curiously. "We could be done with looking at the trees in half the time, except you keep stopping every ten seconds to look for someone."

"I think Mr. Bells might be here," Tayde confided.

Frankie's eyes widened. "Really? How do you know? What does he look like?"

"He texted me some cryptic comment about being here, but he didn't answer when I asked how to find him." She hadn't mentioned it to Frankie before because she knew her friend would immediately abandon all pretense of interest in the trees and focus on launching a search.

"He could be anyone!" Frankie responded gleefully. "Why didn't you tell me sooner? Let's go over to the tables. If he's here, he'll need food at some point."

Tayde followed, but she couldn't eat. She was too anxious. Instead, she simply followed Frankie around, letting her theorize that every particularly unattractive man over the age of seventy "might be him."

Unfortunately, she didn't need Frankie's help. To Tayde, every man in the room looked at her a little strangely. Whereas any one of them could be Mr. Bells, in Tayde's agitated mind, they all were. Part of her wanted to run and hide, while the other part wanted to start canvassing and directly ask any man she encountered if he'd majored in English in college.

Tayde glanced at her phone, checking for any new texts. The blank screen suddenly gave her an idea. "Hey, Frankie," she whispered. "What if I just called him? If someone reaches for his phone, we'll know it's him."

"Tayde, that's brilliant! But you don't have the guts to do it. Hand me your phone. I'll make the call, and you can watch to see who answers."

"I have the guts!" Tayde protested, offended.

"No, you don't. You wouldn't text him before. Knox had to do it."

"That's different," Tayde disagreed, slightly offended.

Frankie lifted her eyebrows expectantly as if waiting for Tayde to prove her wrong.

Tayde glanced at her phone clutched in her hand and hesitated. "Maybe I'll wait until the end of the night. I don't want to interrupt. But if I haven't heard from him—"

"Give me the phone, Tayde." Frankie held out her hand for it, her tone stern.

"No. Not now," Tayde insisted. "Later."

Frankie made a grab for it. "Give me the—"

A loud voice sounded over the room, silencing all talk and activity. "Ladies and Gentlemen. If everyone can come to the stage area, we have a few important announcements before we start the dancing and the rest of our evening."

Frankie glared at Tayde but obediently moved toward the stage. Tayde followed her but hung toward the back. She didn't want to be in the throng of people crowding the front.

The microphone was handed to a stately man who looked to be in his late fifties. After seeing everyone in masks, it was almost startling to see someone's face. "Good evening!" he greeted. "I'm Russ Devoe, founder and CEO of Devonce Investments. Let's pretend I already gave a very eloquent welcome and thanked all the sponsors and countless hardworking, dedicated people who made tonight happen."

Devoe rubbed his hands together in anticipation. "With that out of the way, let's get to the good stuff! I'd like to tell you the story of a woman I credit with saving my company many years ago. Many of you remember a scandal that involved Devonce Investments about fifteen years ago. I never had anything to hide then, and I've never shied away from talking about it since. What you don't know is that the investigative reporter who broke that story is here with us today. Unbeknownst to me at the time, Sheryl investigated my company based on some rumors she came across in her work with a local newspaper. She doggedly researched every employee of my company—including me— putting herself in dangerous situations to locate the truth. And the truth came out in an article that changed my world."

Devoe paused as if overcome by emotion. He was clearly a showman. Every pause and lilt of his voice seemed carefully designed for maximum impact on his audience. He cast a serious look of determination out at the crowd and confessed, "Sheryl Sutton found fraud in my company—fraud I wasn't aware of. More importantly, she found who was responsible. That person was brought to justice, and I was launched into a battle to save my company. It took a lot of effort to rebuild the trust Devonce lost through the actions of one individual and the incompetence of others, including myself. Yes, I was responsible for not keeping a better watch on my own company, and I've spent the last fifteen years rebuilding every last brick myself."

His voice grew stronger and more confident, echoing his company's rise from the ashes. "Ask me any detail of my company today, and I can give you an answer and provide a lengthy paper trail to back it up. That story launched Ms. Sutton's career, and she's spent the last fifteen years as an investigative reporter, traveling the world and bringing more truth to us here back home. You can't imagine my delight when I heard Ms. Sutton was returning to Brighton Falls to captain a magazine. I knew without a doubt it would be a success under her leadership. And... you can't imagine my delight today when I officially announce that Devonce Investments has acquired Chronicle Magazine. We've come full circle, haven't we Sheryl? Devonce is excited to support you in your vision.

"I look forward to watching your continued leadership as

you guide Chronicle to a national and international audience. Now please join me in welcoming and congratulating Devonce's editor-in-chief for Chronicle Media, Sheryl Sutton."

Tayde had been familiar with Sheryl's background. The exposé she'd written uncovering the evils of Devonce Investments had shocked the nation. Sheryl's article and the subsequent law enforcement investigation had cleared Mr. Devoe of wrongdoing beyond naivete about his own company.

Tayde had no idea before tonight that the company acquiring Chronicle was Devonce. Yet, she clapped heartily with everyone else, feeling a sense of poetic justice that the story started so long ago had returned for a happy epilogue.

Looking thrilled, Sheryl dramatically removed her elaborate red mask and accepted the microphone. She was dressed in a flashy red gown designed for attention. She wore it well, but its plunging neckline was something Tayde would never feel comfortable wearing herself.

"A writer by trade, yet I have no words to describe how this feels!" Sheryl spoke confidently, appearing more animated than Tayde had ever seen her. A poised, charismatic public speaker had somehow replaced Tayde's moody boss.

"I knew when I accepted the job, it would be a tough task to turn the magazine around," she continued. "I had no idea it could be accomplished in such a short time or that a company like Devonce would see the potential and partner with us for the future. My employees will tell you I'm a tough boss, but I give credit when credit is due. We would not be here today without Tayde Wright and her mysterious Mr. Bells. When I arrived at the magazine, Tayde was a wannabe writer, and I was desperate. I saw her potential when she couldn't see it herself. I got the idea for a modern-day advice column, and Tayde had the perfect name. I forced her to write *Wrongs Made Wright*, spelled w-r-i-g-h-t, of course. Then a little magic happened. While riding the coattails of Tayde's column, we brought the rest of the magazine up to par. We are now poised to take Tayde and Chronicle to a wider audience with more unique content and headlines to make you click. Please join me in a round of applause to celebrate everything we have accomplished and everything we will accomplish together!"

Tayde was floored by the attention. It was so unexpected, and she felt awkward as the eyes of the room focused on her. Never did she think Sheryl would give her public credit. Now that it happened, Tayde felt overwhelmed. If Sheryl was acting, she was giving an Oscar-worthy performance.

Fortunately, they didn't call Tayde up to the stage, and the blush-inducing attention passed quickly. Sheryl handed the microphone back to Russ Devoe, shifting the focus away from her. Mr. Devoe launched into the thanks and special recognitions he'd glossed over before the announcement. Tayde zoned out, hearing the tenor of his voice but not the individual words.

Then a different sound approached in the background—a subtle tinkling of bells.

"Can I borrow you for a moment, Tayde?" the voice came close and for her ears only.

She turned swiftly, finding a tall, dark-haired man beside her. He wore a plain black mask to match his suit. She couldn't see his face, but his clear blue eyes were kind.

It was him.

He'd called her by name, and the way he'd said it sounded personal, more than if a stranger were addressing her.

She nodded.

He turned and walked toward the doors leading to the outside veranda, and Tayde followed him. Accompanying his steps was the same soft tinkling sound that had first caught her attention.

He stepped outside and held the door for her. She nervously looked around first, making sure there were still people around. Frankie had been closer to the stage, and Tayde hadn't told her where she was going. Tayde wasn't one to go off alone with a strange man. And this one hadn't exactly confessed to being Mr. Bells.

But there was no problem with a conversation in a public place. Feeling assured that there were enough other witnesses who were also escaping the boring speech inside, Tayde stepped out into the night air. The entire area was well lit, revealing elegant lights and Christmas décor festooning the covered area above and glimpses of the tall downtown buildings surrounding them. It was a quiet, romantic setting, though the cold temperatures chased away all but a few visitors. After the noise and brightness inside, the soft, diffused lighting was such a relief that Tayde didn't mind the cold.

Tayde wrapped her fluffy white jacket tighter around her and followed the tinkling bells to a corner, away from everyone else yet still in clear view.

He turned around and faced her. Neither said a word, but each studied the other. Tayde took in his height, the elegant black tux covering broad shoulders, the way his dark hair waved off his forehead, and the kind, glacier-blue eyes studying her just as intently. Her heart pounded, and she had no idea why.

Finally, still not taking his eyes off her, he said, "You're more beautiful in person than in print."

"We finally meet after six months, and that's the best you got?" Tayde's voice sounded breathless.

His eyes crinkled in humor. "Unlike you, I'm better in print than in person. You're sure to be disappointed with the real-life version."

"Who are you?" Tayde asked directly. If what he said was true, she wanted to know who she was to be disappointed in.

"Oh, sorry. Where are my manners? I forgot to introduce myself." He held out his hand formally. "I'm Mr. Bells."

She might have wondered at his sanity but caught the light of humor in his eyes. He was teasing her.

But she would have none of it. "Seriously? You're still not going to tell me?"

His eyes turned serious, and he replied thoughtfully. "No. I don't think I will."

"I don't understand," she protested. "Who are you? Why are you here? Why have you spent the last six months tormenting me? Answer something... anything."

He just looked at her, his eyes shadowed and his lips behind the mask silent.

"Look, if you just came here to look at me, I'm done." Tayde turned to leave.

"Tayde, wait."

It wasn't that he said her name. That wasn't enough to stop her. It was the way he said it. She'd heard a whisper of it the first time he'd said her name at the back of the crowd. She'd thought it familiar and personal. But now... it was almost like a caress. Gentle, loving, and intimate.

She froze. She didn't turn back around but stopped and waited for her heartbeat to calm. It would do no good to turn around and look at him. She couldn't see his face. And she desperately longed to see his face.

She heard his footstep, and then his voice was close, right over her shoulder.

"I never wanted to torment you, Tayde. What you don't

realize is that I'm your biggest fan. Normally, if I see a crazy headline I take issue with, I scroll right on by. It's like propaganda. It's excessive, dramatic, and designed to elicit a strong emotional response. It purposely manipulates readers' emotions like playdough. But your writing was different. I didn't agree with everything you said, but I couldn't fault the intelligence behind it. Your writing was genuine. I responded to your column because your writing is worthy of responding to."

His words beckoned her, and she turned to find him right behind her, but she had no desire to step away. Softly, she spoke, "I was never upset by what you wrote or even that you wrote it. Your comments made me feel stupid. Because you were right. Every single time. You thought of an angle I'd never considered. You pointed out that I'd hurt people, and I felt ashamed. I assumed you must think about me everything I thought of myself. I thought you responded because you didn't like me."

"No, Tayde. I very much liked you. I just wanted to talk to you. I wanted to share my thoughts and then hear yours. That's why I'm here tonight. I wanted to meet you and find out if the reality of you came anywhere close to the Tayde Wright I'd imagined. Would the real Tayde be nearly as kind, talented, and intelligent as the one in print?"

"And what do you think?" she whispered.

She watched his eyes flitter to her hair and around the curve of her face. She saw him swallow.

Then came the soft caress of his voice. "I've always had a great imagination, but nothing compares to the reality of you."

Tayde's eyes locked with his, and she had the strongest desire to touch him. To touch the little lock of hair that fell forward on his forehead. Or maybe to just place her hand gently on the front of his tux. Was he flesh and blood or simply a mirage?

But she couldn't know for sure. "I don't know your name. You're literally hiding behind a mask. If that's how you feel, then why won't you tell me who you are?"

A pained expression furrowed his brow, and he looked away. With it, the spell was broken. Tayde took a step back, putting cold air between them.

When he looked at her again, he looked tormented. "Because then you won't look for me."

"Tayde, there you are!" Frankie came rushing up. "I've been looking everywhere for you. Sheryl is freaking out. She needs you right now."

"Why is Sheryl freaking?" Tayde asked, frantically wondering if she'd done something wrong.

Frankie pursed her lips thoughtfully. "It's not freaking in the bad sense. Everybody's talking. Asking where you are. You need to get in there."

"Just a minute," she said. "Let me finish up with... Frankie, where's that man I was just talking to?"

"What man?" Frankie asked, looking around in confusion.

"He was just here." Tayde spun around, but nobody was behind her. Then she turned a full circle but found no man in a tux.

"He must have left," Frankie latched onto her arm. "That makes it easy. Let's go."

Tayde took a step and heard the sound of tinkling bells. Excited, she looked around, searching every shadow for its source. But there was no one. She took another step and heard more bells. With every movement, the sound came.

She reached into the pocket of her fur jacket and found something round. She drew it out and opened her hand to the light. Two little bells shone back.

Frankie tugged on her arm impatiently.

Tayde turned and looked behind her one last time, concluding that the bells' previous owner must have escaped down the stairs in the corner.

Sighing, she allowed Frankie to pull her toward the door. But then her mind caught up, and she stopped her right before they reached it. "What's going on?" she asked. "Why is everyone talking? What did I miss?"

"Mr. Bells' comment, of course," Frankie replied simply.

"What comment? Tayde asked, anxiety beginning to churn in her stomach. "He hasn't commented since the food column."

Frankie replied tightly, "No, he just commented. On the school column."

Tayde's stomach somersaulted, and she fumbled for her phone.

"That's impossible," Tayde protested, instantly latching onto denial. "He couldn't have commented right now. I was just talking to him." Frankie must be wrong. Or maybe that wasn't the real Mr. Bells.

Frankie shrugged. "He probably did it earlier, but because of the party, no one noticed until now. Sheryl is freaking out because she wants everyone to run back to the office right now, get the new post with his comment up, and set up advertising."

Tayde brought up the magazine's website, still feeling complete denial. "Right now? But it's Saturday night, and we're at a Christmas party."

"Now you understand the freaking," Frankie said dryly.

This wasn't happening. He wouldn't do that. He would have mentioned it if he'd posted something before coming to the party. He wouldn't have gone behind her back. He wouldn't have said any of those beautiful words.

Frankie's hand came over her phone screen. "Um... Tayde,

maybe you shouldn't do that right now. Just go talk to Sheryl. Then we'll leave. Wait to read it until then."

Tayde felt the blood drain from her face. Frankie's reaction could only mean one thing. The comment was bad. Really bad.

She turned away from her friend, and Frankie's hand fell harmlessly off Tayde's screen. With her cold, shaking fingers, Tayde scrolled through over a week's worth of positive comments until she reached one at the end.

First, she checked the time. Sure enough. The comment was posted earlier. Tayde guessed he'd posted it right before he'd asked to speak to her.

While Frankie stood impatiently by in the cold, Tayde read the letter. She felt her face alternately burn and become deathly pale. She finished reading it and began to scroll back up to reread it, but Frankie stopped her.

"Reread it later, Tayde. You need to go deal with Sheryl. In case you didn't notice, she texted you three times while you were reading."

Tayde fumbled with her phone, feeling the threat of tears. "I don't understand. There's no way he could have gotten that information. Knox was the teacher."

"Wait. Knox was the teacher?" Frankie sputtered.

"Yes. There's no way he could have gotten that personal information unless he…." Tayde's voice trailed off as an absurd, nightmarish idea popped into her mind.

Ignoring Frankie's protests, she read the letter again, her mind quickly dissecting every detail. By the time she finished, she knew with certainty what had happened. And she'd never felt such betrayal.

Knox.

Dear Ms. Wright,

I agree with everything you so eloquently stated in your most recent column.

While I do not want to detract in any way from your well-stated points, I would like to add to the discussion with another perspective. Sometimes the story on the surface is not the only story. Sometimes, the less obvious story also needs a voice.

Your powerful column does not relate the events leading up to the boy's unfortunate reaction of throwing a chair. When the student arrived at class that day, he inadvertently knocked over a chair. Since it was an accident, he didn't bother picking it up but took a different seat. A group of girls then proceeded to harass and humiliate him, insisting that he pick up the chair.

You were correct that the student in question has known anger issues. Regardless of that (or maybe because of it), the girls continued their verbal assault. He refused to pick up the chair. In fact, he refused to say anything. But after such unrelenting pressure, he threw a pencil in anger. A warning shot, if you will.

Having solicited that mild reaction, the girls terrorized him further, chastising and ridiculing him until he could no longer control his anger. He threw the chair. He didn't aim it at anyone. He didn't intend to hurt anyone. He simply wanted the anger and abuse directed at him to end.

Unlike my previous letter, these are not possibly fictional events. This is a factual account of what occurred as reported by another student in the class. The witness stated that he felt bad for the boy who got in trouble because "the girls kinda deserved it. They wouldn't leave him alone." However, because this boy has "known anger *issues," there was no investigation into—why—he blew up or the events leading to the incident. All the blame was put on him, while no one who incited him admitted or accepted any responsibility.*

I adamantly believe we need to do everything necessary to allow our kids to learn in safety. As you already stated, we need to reassess how we handle challenging issues that pose risks and find a balance where all students access their educational rights while not interfering with the safety and educational rights of others. However, situations are unique, and you cannot prescribe a one-size-fits-all solution that overlooks the individual person and his or her needs. While striving for better protocols, let us also prioritize caring and empathy. Let's look at each situation as unique and work to investigate the causes instead of simply treating the results.

The boy in the incident probably cannot present his own case of what happened that day. He cannot lift his own voice in defense of his actions. Instead, he needed another student, a witness, to report it for him. He needed an advocate. And I'm happy to report that now he has more than one.

Since the incident, the teacher met with the student witness and thanked him for being brave enough to come forward with the truth and advocate for someone who needed it, someone others overlooked. He assigned seating in the classroom and placed the boy with anger issues at a table with the witness and his friends. They are kind to him and appreciate that he is smart. The girls were tactfully confronted about their actions and now sit on the opposite side of the room. There have been no further incidents.

Let's be the whisper of change. But let's always be the voice of the silent.

Can you hear the bells?

Chapter Thirteen

Tayde slammed the door of her apartment and leaned her back against it. She'd held things together until now. Frankie had been so concerned that she'd made Tayde promise not to do anything until she arrived at her apartment. She'd even followed Tayde home, ensuring her friend safely made it there.

Now that Tayde was here, her hands shook with emotion. She didn't know where to start. She felt betrayed by both Knox and Mr. Bells. It was late, but she knew she wouldn't be able to sleep until she confronted them.

Her phone beeped. She looked at the notification.

```
Mr. Bells: Are you okay?
```

She pushed the button to dial his number. She heard the line click to connect the call.

"No, I'm not okay!" she seethed. "The entire time you spoke to me and told me how much you liked me, you knew! You knew you'd posted a reply, you'd used my brother to stab me in the back, and you had the nerve to tell me how much you *liked* me!"

"Everything I said to you was true." Mr. Bells' voice was soft and calm.

"But you didn't tell me the whole truth," Tayde accused hotly. "Withholding pertinent information is the same as lying. The result is you deceived me. You told me one thing while your actions said something else entirely."

"That's rather ironic." For the first time, Mr. Bells sounded upset, even angry. "You're accusing me of lying even though you deceived everyone when you impersonated someone else and wrote your own reader letter."

Tayde's breath caught, feeling a new level of betrayal. "Knox told you!" There was no other way he could have known.

"Knox didn't breathe a word," Bells' voice was taut and crisp. "It was obvious. The reader was entirely your style. It had you written all over it."

Tayde saw what he was doing. It was a classic diversion technique designed to direct attention away from someone who'd done something wrong and shift it to someone who'd supposedly done a much worse wrong. Tayde slipped off her heels and flung them onto the couch.

"Don't turn this around," she bit out. "I'm not the one who was wrong here. You went behind my back and turned my brother against me. You publicly humiliated me again and did it while playing me the fool."

"Tayde, the letter wasn't about you!" His voice came fierce and insistent.

Tayde scoffed, "It was all about me! How did you know Knox was the teacher in the letter? How did you know I even had a brother? Are you spying on me?"

"Come on, Tayde. It wasn't that hard." His voice lost the edge of anger and instead sounded almost patronizing. "You wrote the letter for him. That was obvious. I have certain resources available to me. It wasn't hard to research your family and find out that your brother is a teacher."

"You researched me?" Tayde paused in her pacing across the floor. He'd said it as if it were a normal thing.

"Of course," he replied easily. With his emotions now under control, Bells returned to his usual calm, soft-spoken manner. "I was fascinated by your column. I wondered what had triggered the boy in the classroom. When I learned you had a brother, I wanted to contact him anyway. Knox told me what had really happened, and I knew it needed to be told. I tried not to detract from the important message in your letter. I wish you could see it's about more than you."

Now he was calling her self-centered. Tayde couldn't reason beyond her emotions. It wouldn't matter what Bells said. She wouldn't hear it. All she knew was the shock, pain, and embarrassment of being betrayed by both her brother and a man who'd professed to care.

"I'm not a big fan of the 'it's not personal, it's business' cliché." Her words strained with bitterness. "What you did was personal."

"I didn't intend to hurt you," he said quietly.

She labeled his words as an excuse. What someone intends to do doesn't matter. The reality is that she was so hurt it felt like physical pain. Never once had Bells apologized. Instead, he'd insinuated that she was deceitful and self-centered. And his calm, soft words made her feel even worse—like she was overly dramatic and wrong.

She momentarily wobbled between reacting in anger or

breaking down in tears.

But anger didn't hurt so bad.

"I know you didn't *intend* anything." She breathlessly threw out the words like hard rocks thrown in his direction. "But the reality is a whole lot different than you intended. So, I will give you the courtesy you didn't give me. I will tell you exactly what I *intend* to do. I will find you. I will search until I find your name, occupation, and every last detail of your life. Like you've said, everyone has his or her own story, and we've all been the villain in someone's eyes. You write about others' stories without ever mentioning anything of your own. What are you hiding? When I find out who you are, I intend to publish your story with all its dark secrets and let everyone see the man behind the curtain."

His reply was quiet and sad, barely audible over Tayde's heavy breathing. "I hope you do, Tayde. I hope you do."

Tayde's finger shook as she ended the call.

She knew if she stopped to breathe for ten seconds, she'd lose her composure and crumple into a heap. She couldn't do that now. She wasn't finished.

She marched to Knox's bedroom and flipped the light switch. The room immediately filled with light, illuminating an unmoving heap under a blanket on the bed. Tayde took three strides and snatched the edge of the blanket, tugging it off to reveal Knox's sleeping form.

"Knox Wright, what did you do?" she demanded.

"Went to bed," he answered groggily. "Leave me alone. I'm sleeping." He pulled his pillow over his head.

Tayde grabbed the pillow and pulled until it came flying out of her brother's grip. Then she threw it at him.

"Get up, Knox! I don't feel bad one bit. You're never in bed at this time on a Saturday night."

"I am when I'm trying to hide from you!" he grumbled. "Go

away, Tayde!"

Tayde grabbed another pillow and reared her hand back to fire it.

"I won't!" she hissed. "You owe me an explanation! I saw the letter, Knox!"

Suddenly, the fight drained out of her. The memory of her conversation with Mr. Bells collided with the memory of what had started it all. And she ran out of anger. The pillow fell from her hands, and her legs turned to mush. She slid down to the floor with her fancy dress puffed up around her and her back against the bed. She pulled her knees to her chest and bowed her head to the folds of her skirt. "I saw the letter," she repeated, a sob catching in her throat.

Her tears achieved what her anger never could. Knox sat up in bed with a miserable moan.

"Aw, Tayde!" he groaned. "Don't do that! I'm sorry!"

"You talked to him, Knox!" Tayde sobbed, her words barely distinguishable. "You gave him all that information—stuff you never told me even though you knew I was writing the column. Then, you never bothered to mention that you'd even talked to him!"

Knox slid off the bed onto the floor beside her, his back against the mattress alongside hers. "I know what it looks like. But that's not how it was, Tayde. Why do you think I've been so miserable all week? I wanted to tell you. He never said I shouldn't tell you. But I could never work up the nerve. I knew you'd be mad. I just waited until his letter came out and hoped you'd see the full story and not be as mad. I guess I was wrong."

"I'm not mad about the kid," Tayde said. She reached out and took Knox's hand in her cold one. Her brother was her best friend. Though she was hurt, nothing would change that. "Why on earth didn't you tell me? How awful for that boy who was harassed until he lost control! Didn't you consider that pertinent information when you told me the story?"

"I didn't know," Knox rushed to explain. "The morning after it happened—after I told you and you decided to turn it into a column—a student came to talk to me before school. He told me everything I should have known and didn't. He told me about what the group of girls had done and how they provoked the other student until he threw the chair. Tayde, I felt awful. I was in the hallway when it happened, but I should have paid closer attention to the classroom. Or I should have asked questions and investigated instead of simply assuming all fault lay with the obvious. I immediately tried to contact you and tell you not to run the column until I talked to you. But it was too late. Your column had already been posted."

"So, you thought the next best thing was to give the story to Mr. Bells so he could show me up?" Tayde asked. Though she appreciated his explanation, he'd had other options.

Knox wearily reached up and rubbed his temple. "Your column came out on Friday, the same day I heard the real story from my student. Since it was too late to make a difference in your column, I didn't tell you the new information. I knew it would upset you, and there was no point. My thirteen-year-old student and I were the only ones who knew the truth. But then Mr. Bells contacted me on Monday. I don't know how he found me, but he sent me an email and asked me to call him."

"You didn't have to call," Tayde moaned dramatically. "Why did you call?"

Knox looked at her incredulously. "Because this guy had driven my sister nuts for months! I thought if I talked to him, I might get some clues to help you figure out who he is. So, I called him. He's a nice guy, Tayde. Before I knew what was happening, I'd told him the whole story. I didn't intend to tell him, but he coaxed it out of me. I'm sorry you were hurt and felt like I went behind your back, but I'm glad I told him. It was the right thing to do."

"You knew he was going to respond to my column?" she asked, wondering if Bells had tricked Knox. If so, that gave her yet another reason to hate him.

"Yes, I did," Knox said firmly, accepting responsibility and dashing Tayde's hopes in the process. "He was pretty blunt about his intentions. At first, I got angry and told him he couldn't use the information I'd told him."

"But you changed your mind?" Obviously. The column was published. Though Knox regretted hurting her, he clearly didn't regret Bells writing the letter.

Knox nodded. "Bells asked me what the right thing to do was. He asked me if it was fair to my student and all the students like him to keep their stories silent. He asked me if it would be worth it if reading the real story made things better for one kid. He said my student had been a voice for someone who couldn't speak for himself. He asked if I would allow him to be a voice too."

Tayde shifted uncomfortably, starting to feel the stiffness of sitting on the floor. "But if you'd just told me, I could have written a follow-up myself."

"I told Mr. Bells that," Knox assured. "But then he asked me if I thought you would. The magazine doesn't let you write what you want, Tayde. You've never been allowed to respond directly to Bells, and he knows that. In the end, even if you wanted to write the real story, you wouldn't be allowed to. You've never followed up on a story. Bells said he was in the unique position to tell the truth and get it the attention it deserved. Think about it, Tayde. A follow-up letter from you would not get the attention that a response from Mr. Bells gets.

I had to let him write it. My student, and all students like him, deserve to have their perspective acknowledged and valued."

Tayde sighed and boosted herself up to sit on the edge of the mattress, a far more comfortable position, especially in a full gown. Likewise, she resigned herself to giving up her anger for the more comfortable position of forgiveness. As much as she hated it, Tayde couldn't fault Knox. She hadn't asked his permission to write about the incident in the first place. He'd asked her not to. She'd written the letter on his behalf despite his reservations.

In the end, Knox had done what he thought best for his students. And if she had to take the hit for it, then it was a price she was willing to pay. Bells had been correct in saying that it wasn't about her. Now that the red haze of anger began to recede, other more rational thoughts and emotions competed for her attention. Bells' letter had been heartbreaking, beautiful, and so necessary. Her heart hurt that she'd missed the deeper truth, but she knew she couldn't have written it better. He'd been right. Even if she'd been allowed to write a follow-up, it wouldn't have carried the same weight and attention. Bells was the one who needed to tell it, even if it painted her as the villain once more.

"I just wish you would have told me," Tayde said tiredly. "I knew something was wrong. You've been moping around all week. But you didn't tell me." She was grasping at straws to find one thing to justify the remnants of hurt she still felt. It was a bitter pill to realize that, though you were hurt by someone, you understood.

"I'm sorry, Tayde," Knox responded, showing no hesitation in his apology. He wrapped his arm around her shoulder and pulled her close. "I should have told you that he'd contacted me and was writing the response. But I knew how you'd react. I hated the situation, but I didn't want you to do anything to prevent him from posting. He's texted me a couple of times this week. He took his time writing it and praying about it. He was really worried about your reaction."

"Do you know who he is?" she asked, voicing the question that replayed incessantly through her mind.

Knox shook his head. "No, he never told me. I never asked. He really is like a Robin Hood. If I pulled off his mask, would he be able to continue the good he's accomplished? As far as I'm concerned, the man can keep his secret identity."

"So, I'm just supposed to let him continue anonymously responding to my columns and making me look bad?" Tayde asked. It didn't seem fair. He knew who she was, but she had no information about him.

"I think he'll eventually tell you," Knox assured. "He's a really good guy, Tayde. I don't know who he is, and I don't understand his Robin Hood motivation. I don't know why he feels compelled to respond to you. Maybe you both share the same compulsion to right the world's wrongs. But I know he cares. He cares about others. He cares about justice. And he cares about you."

"He doesn't even know me," Tayde said skeptically. She thought back to her phone call earlier. "Even if he did care, I'm sure I cured that issue now. I didn't exactly treat him well after I read his letter. I was upset."

"Did you wake him from a dead sleep and rip the covers off his bed to chew him out?" Knox asked.

"Something like that," Tayde said demurely. She didn't want to share. She didn't even want to think about it.

"I think you're safe," Knox assured. "Look at this." Knox pulled out his phone and pushed the screen several times to bring up his text messages. Then he handed the phone to Tayde.

```
Bells: Is she ok?
```

Tayde looked at the time stamp and realized the message had been sent only a few minutes ago. As she watched, another text message appeared.

```
Bells: Can't sleep. Need to know she's ok.
```

"What do you think?" Knox asked. "Should we put the poor guy out of his misery?"

"I don't even know what to say to him." A new emotion entered the mix: shame. She felt ashamed of how she'd reacted. "I don't think I can face him, not tonight. And by 'face,' I mean figuratively. I've never seen the man's actual face."

"No worries. I'll take care of it." His fingers flew across the screen.

"Wait. What are you texting? Let me see. Knox!"

He clicked send and handed the phone to her. "There you go."

```
Knox: The hulk has lost her angry green and
returned to Tayde. Feels bad. Talk later.
```

"Knox! I didn't want you to say that!"

"Say what? That you turned green with anger or that you'll talk to him later?"

"Both! I can't talk to him." Even though she understood, she didn't know that she ever wanted to talk to him again.

Knox shrugged. "You'll figure it out. Can I go back to bed now?"

Tayde stood. "Thanks, Knox. Sweet dreams."

She shut off the light as she left and went to her bedroom. She took off her dress, noting the tear stains. She showered, readied for bed, and finally crawled under the sheets. But even though she was exhausted, she knew she had no hope of sleeping. Her body felt the remnants of a large amount of adrenaline, and she was too jittery to relax.

She glanced at her phone, debating if she should just text Mr. Bells an apology. But she couldn't bring herself to do it. Maybe tomorrow.

Instead, she pulled her laptop to the bed and opened it up. If she couldn't sleep, she might as well work. She had another column due soon and hadn't yet chosen a reader letter to respond to.

A long list of new messages awaited her. Most of them were letters forwarded by Sheryl. Her boss never allowed her access to the magazine's email. Instead, she would forward the pertinent letters or else add them to a shared folder. Tayde often wondered if Sheryl weeded through them first before they made it to Tayde.

She glanced through them quickly, but they only made Tayde feel more discouraged. Nothing inspired her. With the trauma still fresh from Mr. Bells' response, everything she read felt too "dangerous."

She scrolled back up to the top, one email catching her eyes. It was sent directly to Tayde's account and hadn't been filtered through Sheryl or the magazine's general public contact email. She didn't recognize the sender's address, but the subject caught her attention: Try Making this Wrong Wright.

She clicked on it, and the email filled her screen.

Dear Chronicle,

I think you should know you just sold out to the Devil himself. It's ironic that though you profess to "wright the wrongs" of the world, you were just acquired by a wrong that was never righted.

Maybe you should look into what happened fifteen years ago. The Devonce Investments fraud scandal was tied up in a pretty bow. Sheryl Sutton was the hero. Russ Devoe was the victim. And the villain was a low-level bookkeeper who spent the rest of his life in prison. Now Devoe gets to return the favor and buy Sutton's magazine. Awfully convenient, isn't it?

Your magazine column proclaims to look deeper and tell the story behind the story. You are a voice for the underdog. Maybe you should look a little closer to home at your own story.

Don't worry. I know you won't. Conspiracy theories are crazy, right? I've followed your columns but not anymore. You should be known by the company you keep. I cannot trust an organization of hypocrites.

Good luck with your next endeavors. May you continue to fleece the public as effectively as Devonce did fifteen years ago. God help those you manipulate to fit the story you want to tell. Your version of 'right' is not right. The term I use for it is 'wrong.'

Sincerely,
Disgusted with a bunch of hypocrites

Tayde read through the email twice. Tayde noticed that the letter was not directed to her specifically, but it was sent to her personally. She could feel the hostility of the writer. Angry emails were not new, but they usually complained about someone else, not the magazine. Maybe there had been others Sheryl had never let her see. When someone else controlled your information, you couldn't guarantee its validity or completeness.

This was a dangerous reader letter. Sheryl would never let her respond to something that painted the magazine in an unfavorable light. It wasn't an option, and she knew better than to ask. It sounded as if the reader was just angry and blaming Devonce for the bad things that had befallen him or her. Probably a disgruntled employee. Classic abdicating responsibility rather than recognizing the consequences of personal actions.

But what if she did respond... Not publicly, of course. But the idea was fascinating. If she were to write a letter in response, what would she write?

She opened a blank document on her computer. Her mouse hovered, waiting to obey her command. She could write a response. She could probably very kindly validate the writer's feelings while pushing him to recognize that whatever happened in the past was the past. What he does now and what Chronicle does now is new and brimming with the possibilities of bettering the world. She could do it. Even if no one saw it.

But the little arrow on the screen still hovered, and Tayde's fingers froze, poised on the keyboard. Then a thought whispered through her head.

What would Mr. Bells do?

Then she closed the screen and put the laptop away.

This time, she would do things differently.

Chapter Fourteen

Jeff

"Russ, I can't keep doing this. We're going to get caught." Jeff tried to study the spreadsheet in front of him, but the nervous tic in his left eye made it almost impossible.

"Stop being dramatic, Jeff," Russ said, lazily reclining on the couch in the corner as if he were ready for a session with a psychologist. "One more transaction before Christmas won't tip off the feds. Everyone has already left on vacation. It's the perfect time to get some business taken care of."

Jeff had grown accustomed to the ever-present anxiety. Every day, he holed up in his office and prayed no one would find him. For the most part, the other employees of Devonce Investments left him alone. Jeff did his job and kept his head down. But he lived in dread of when Russ made a personal visit. That always meant the matter to be discussed was too sensitive to go through email or over the phone. And today was one such day.

Russ seemed so relaxed and unbothered, completely opposite of everything Jeff felt. His suit was pressed perfectly, and his million-dollar smile flashed in just the right places. But underneath it all, Jeff knew his boss was a snake. Now he had to convince the narcissistic man that his charisma was in danger of running out. If Jeff didn't find a way to fix the problem, no amount of charm could save either one of them.

Jeff turned to his boss and pushed his glasses up his nose. "If I use that amount of money to cover Monroe's withdrawal, I won't have the funds needed to pay the rest of the investors."

Russ waved his hand as if batting away a pesky fly. "They can wait. I have more investors chomping at the bit."

"They *can't* wait," Jeff insisted. "We're supposed to pay their returns by the end of the calendar year, as you promised. If they get impatient and withdraw, we won't have the money to pay what we owe."

Jeff's words finally seemed to sink in. Russ drew his feet down off the couch and sat up. "What if I get a bunch of small investors to buy in within the next few days?" He nodded as if Jeff had already approved of the idea. "Pay Monroe off. I'll get us more cash. Then we'll use that to pay the investors waiting for their returns. Just like we always do."

"That might work," Jeff said grudgingly, hating himself even as he admitted to the possibility of more shady deals. "But the transactions are getting more difficult to hide. Small, infrequent transactions were never a problem. But it's impossible to hide the quantities you're bringing in. With the holidays, I can't distribute the money to both Monroe and the other investors quickly enough, especially when the money doesn't actually exist!"

Russ's handsome face curled with a snarl. "Monroe was an idiot to pull his funds. I can cover it. Text me the exact amount needed. I'm going to a fancy charity fundraiser tonight. I can drum up some business there. No worries. Business is good."

"It's not business, Russ. It's fraud." Jeff didn't usually speak so boldly. His heart felt like it would beat out of his chest. Sweat drenched his forehead. Yes, he was afraid, but he was tired of being afraid.

Taking a deep breath of his stale office air, he continued. "I want out," he said, his voice thin and shaky. "I have to look my wife and kids in the eye. I'm not a thief. Consider this my two weeks' notice."

"No, you aren't a thief, Jeff. I know that," Russ said warmly. He stood and put a hand on Jeff's back in support. "You're a man who loves his family. His wife."

Jeff puffed out his chest. "My wife would be the first to say her health is not worth my integrity."

Russ nodded and raised his hands in surrender. "Ok. You're out. Officially terminated. No severance. Your insurance ends immediately."

Shocked, Jeff shook his head in disbelief. "No, you can't fire me. I'm quitting."

"Oh, no, I'm firing you," Russ said firmly. "We've come across some discrepancies in our books. Our bookkeeper has apparently been laundering a very large amount of money, keeping it in a separate account and not applying it to investments as instructed. I need to turn you in to the authorities, Jeff. I don't have a choice."

Jeff couldn't breathe. His eyes searched Russ frantically, hoping the man would laugh and say he was only kidding. But even in the dim lighting of his office hole, Jeff could see the evil gleam in Russ's eyes.

Jeff swallowed with difficulty. He cleared his throat and choked out, "How do you want me to label the new investments?"

Russ's mouth extended in a grin that could compete with the Cheshire cat. "They are investments in the resort in Mexico."

"There is no resort in Mexico," Jeff said dully.

"Exactly."

Jeff sat back down in his chair and slumped over the computer screen, once again the obedient slave.

Russ pounded him on the back. "Don't worry, Jeff. I'll take care of you. I always have. Remember when Patricia first got sick? That was before we made it to the big time. I fronted you the money out of my own pocket. I've been here every step of the way. Is it true that she might be eligible for a clinical trial? Does insurance cover that? Just remember, I'll take care of you so you can take care of Patricia."

The warning came through loud and clear. Russ was right about helping him. When Patricia first got sick, she'd had to quit her job. Their income took a significant hit. Russ gave him a personal loan so they could pay their mortgage until they got back on their feet. A few months afterward, Russ started requesting that Jeff not record things accurately in the books. In return, Russ canceled Jeff's debt. Since then, Russ had increased Jeff's salary and allowed him to move up in the company. The demands on Jeff's bookkeeping skills had increased, but so had the rewards.

And Russ had just let him know that getting out was not an option.

Jeff nodded and said simply, "Got it."

"Good! Get Monroe paid. I'll let you know when I have the funds to cover everything else. Send me the number!"

Russ left. Jeff's office returned to quiet once again, but Jeff felt no peace. He tried not to think, focusing instead on the numbers swimming in front of him on the screen. He wished he'd never gotten involved with Russ Devoe. But just like everyone else, he'd fallen for the man's charm and extravagant promises. Jeff had jumped at the opportunity to work at a respectable, up-and-coming investment firm. Then Patricia had gotten sick, and before he realized Devonce wasn't respectable at all, he was in too deep to back out. Now he was just as guilty as everyone else.

The difference was that he knew how quickly the house of cards could fall. No one else seemed worried about it. Not everyone knew what was going on, but those who did knew their activities were illegal. They were running the equivalent of a Ponzi scheme. But they'd gotten away with it so far. Russ was right in saying "business" was good. One investor had pulled out at exactly the wrong time, but if Russ could come up with cash in a hurry like he always did, then the house of cards would stay up with no one the wiser.

Jeff turned off his computer the second the clock struck five o'clock. His job was like a daily nightmare. It was time for him to wake up and go home where he could forget all this and focus on a vastly different life.

He walked out of the building with his head down, speaking to no one. Only after he drove across town and opened the front door of his house did he feel the stress loosen its grip.

"Hi, Dad!" came the greeting from his two kids. They were both teenagers but still looked up from their video game long enough to greet him.

"Mom must be making spaghetti!" Jeff said, smelling the

spicy aroma.

"Hey, Dad," his son walked over close and lowered his voice. "Do you really have tomorrow off? Think you could help me finish that garden box I wanted to make for Mom?"

Jeff smiled, feeling relief at the answer he could give. "Yes, I have it off. It's Christmas Eve! And of course, I'll help you. We need to get it done before dinner and presents tomorrow night!"

The spaghetti was soon ready. They sat at the table as a family, and Jeff recited the blessing as usual. But this time, the act of speaking to the Almighty in front of his wife and kids made him feel like a fraud. Jeff opened his eyes and looked around at their happy faces. What would they say if they knew what he'd done? They'd be ashamed of him. He was ashamed of himself. He'd helped steal millions and millions of dollars. This house and everything they had was paid for with money that rightfully belonged to someone else.

He wished he could change things. He wanted to be someone his family could be proud of. But he was trapped. He looked at Patricia, noticing the dark smudges under her eyes and the strain around her mouth that signaled she was in pain, even though she never complained.

The cancer had returned. They hadn't told the kids yet. Jeff had no idea how Russ knew they were discussing the possibility of a clinical trial. But her chances didn't look good. They needed to fight hard, and that fight would cost money. If the choice was his integrity or his wife's life, he'd choose her. For the sake of Patricia and his children, he would do whatever was necessary to get her the best medical care. Unfortunately, it felt like he'd made a deal with the devil himself.

Jeff pushed his anxiety aside. He laughed with his family, and they even played a card game after dinner. The evening felt like an oasis, but by the night's end, Jeff realized it was instead the eye of a hurricane.

He'd just said goodnight to the kids when his phone beeped with a text from Russ.

```
Devoe: Monroe has been talking. Murphy and Dixon
are pulling out. Formally requesting their funds
immediately.
```

Jeff felt ill. Those were some of their largest investors—some of Devoe's friends who had originally fronted the money into Devonce. The house of cards was falling.

```
Jeff: We can't cover that amount.
```

Devoe's reply came quickly.

```
Devoe: Use every penny you can access and pay what
you can tonight. They'll have to wait for the rest.
```

Jeff did as he was told. He logged on with his computer and divided everything in the account between Murphy and Dixon. The amount he paid wasn't nearly what was owed, but the Devonce account was at a zero balance when he finished.

Thankfully, Patricia was already asleep and didn't notice his agitation. His endless tossing and turning didn't even rouse her. Jeff eventually gave up. He got out of bed and went downstairs, hoping that if he couldn't sleep, he could at least relax with a good sci-fi movie.

He'd made it through one Star Wars movie and started another when dawn broke. He saw the light out the window and paused, holding his breath for the instant the sun would peek over the horizon and start the day.

Two seconds before the world breathed, Jeff's phone rang, jumpstarting his heart with a jolt. He fumbled for it with startled, clumsy fingers. A horrible premonition flooded him the instant he saw Russ's name flash on the screen.

"Hello?" Jeff answered.

"Did you see the article? Don't go to the office. The feds are there. Delete everything you can remotely."

"Wait... What?"

But Russ had already ended the call.

Jeff didn't take time to call him back or investigate what he'd meant by "the article." He ran for his computer and began deleting everything, both in the cloud and on his hard drive. With his hands shaking with tremors and waves of nausea threatening, he erased files, emails, and whatever else he could find. It didn't matter if it related to their illegal activities. He deleted it anyway. The worst part was that he knew it wouldn't matter. To someone educated on the subject, the fraud was obvious. There was too much to cover up. Though he could delete a lot, he couldn't delete everything. He didn't have access to the evidence stored elsewhere. Countless emails and bank account discrepancies would all trace back to him. And the fact that he was wiping everything clean wouldn't help his case. But he did it anyway.

Jeff was not sloppy in his record-keeping. He had created ledgers that were fake and ledgers that were real. Though he deleted everything from the computer, he had saved everything and hidden it where it wouldn't be found. It was evidence that both convicted and exonerated him.

The door to his home office squeaked open, and Patricia entered, her face drawn and pale.

She held out the morning newspaper with the cover page blaring the sins of Devonce in large, bold letters. "What is this about, Jeff? It says Devonce is involved in illegal activities. It was written by Sheryl Sutton!"

He accepted the paper, seeing Sheryl's name there in black and white, just like all the facts detailing the fraudulent activities of the supposedly successful investment firm.

He felt hot. Sweat dotted his forehead and ran down his neck. He'd never once lied to his wife, but the words came from his lips anyway. "It's just a misunderstanding. Smoke and mirrors. Russ will sort it out."

"But how could Sheryl do something like that?" Patricia asked, her tone hurt and confused.

Russ and Sheryl had been dating for about a year. The two couples had attended multiple events together. Though Jeff would never label Russ as his friend, Patricia and Sheryl had hit things off and developed a real friendship, at least that's what it seemed. Now Jeff wondered. Had it all been a setup? Had Sheryl dated Russ and gotten close to them just to investigate the company?"

Jeff shrugged and tossed down the paper as if it didn't matter. He never even bothered to read the article. "You know Sheryl. She's driven. She has her sights set on the big leagues and probably saw this as an opportunity to make a splash and get some attention. It doesn't matter if any of it is true or not. Sheryl likes drama."

"But what if people believe her lies?" Worry saturated her voice, and Jeff hated it.

He stood and wrapped his arms around his wife, pulling her close. "It'll be okay. Russ will take care of it. It will be okay." He'd said it twice, trying to convince himself he spoke the truth.

But it didn't work. It was definitely *not* going to be okay. But he couldn't tell her that. He couldn't bear to see the fear, disappointment, and shame. The truth would eventually come out. If just for a few more hours, he wanted Patricia to believe he was a good man.

He held her close, breathing in the fresh scent of her hair and feeling the warmth of her safe in his arms.

Then she pulled away and smiled tremulously. "Let's not think about it now. Let's make it a good Christmas Eve for the kids. I'll start on the pie for tonight if you'll make breakfast."

"Deal." Jeff closed his office door and headed to the kitchen to make pancakes. The rest of the day passed with blissful simplicity, and he could almost believe the article didn't exist. That was not reality. Instead, reality consisted of making pancakes, helping his son finish the garden box for his mom, playing card games, and eating Christmas cookies.

His phone rang repeatedly, but he didn't answer. Finally, he turned it off. He'd done all he could. He knew it wasn't enough. But he was going to cling to his façade of normal until it fell down around him.

Traditionally, they opened one present on Christmas Eve, usually after dinner. However, the kids started nagging in the afternoon. Even though they were teenagers, their excitement for Christmas was childlike and contagious. Jeff couldn't resist. With dinner a few minutes from being done, he granted their request, and they all gathered around the tree.

"This is the only one!" he said, giving his standard announcement. "Everything else waits for the morning." He handed them each a gift. Patricia looked startled when he handed her a gift too. Mom and Dad didn't usually participate in the Christmas Eve gifts, but Jeff didn't want to wait. He'd gotten her a ring with their children's birthstones in it. He couldn't wait to see her open it.

The doorbell rang.

Patricia glanced at the clock. "Who could that be? It's

Christmas Eve!"

"Maybe it's Santa!" their daughter, Maya, giggled.

But Jeff knew any visitor wasn't going to bring tidings of joy. He jumped up and said a little too enthusiastically, "I'll get it. Let's just pause the presents for just a minute."

He didn't know what he expected to find, but opening the door to multiple police officers was still shocking.

"Mr. Bennett, we're here to place you under arrest."

He stepped forward slightly and lowered his voice to the man who seemed in charge. "Please. Not in front of my kids."

The man's gaze flickered up behind Jeff's shoulder, and he gave a slight nod.

Jeff raised his voice and said lightly, "I'm going to go with these gentlemen for a bit. You all go ahead and eat dinner."

He glanced behind him to see his wife and children watching with wide, shocked eyes.

Jeff forced a smile. "No worries. Just need to straighten some things out. It will be okay."

He stepped through the door and down the sidewalk. A pair of handcuffs were placed on his wrists. A monotone voice recited his rights, though Jeff couldn't recall any of the actual words. All he could think about was getting the process over quickly, ending the nightmarish scene his family was surely witnessing. He ducked into the police car and waited for the car to pull away from the curb.

He didn't want to look back and see his family's anguish. He didn't want that image engraved in his mind.

But he looked anyway.

In front of the gray house with a red door stood three figures. Their pale faces twisted with horror, and their hands clutched unopened Christmas presents.

Chapter Fifteen

Tayde

Tayde read the email for at least the fiftieth time. She wished she could just let it go. But it bothered her. The words had continued on repeat twenty-four hours a day since the night she read it the first time. She'd written another column and published it. She was supposed to be working on another one. She wasn't going to touch this email with a ten-foot pole. She'd never even considered it. But still, it plagued her.

"Hey, Tayde." Frankie ducked into Tayde's cubicle. "I need to find out your plans for the next few columns. Sheryl is nagging me to update the website with Christmas designs and promos for 'Wrongs Made Wright Christmas Edition.'"

"I've got nothing," Tayde said honestly, feeling the anxiety creeping up. She needed three more Christmas-themed columns, with the last one to be posted on Christmas Eve. She hadn't chosen reader letters. She didn't even have a theme. She couldn't get her brain to move on from the one email that plagued her.

Frankie perched on the table beside Tayde's desk. "Maybe I can help. I'm always good for crazy ideas."

"I don't lack choices," Tayde sighed, bringing up a long list of emails to scroll through. "Plenty of complaints to keep me busy, and more coming in all the time. But there's nothing here I want to write about."

"So, what do you want to write?" Frankie asked. "Just say the word, and I'll write an anonymous reader letter, and we're all set!"

Tayde irritably scrolled through her messages, mentally categorizing the letters. So many of them were disgustingly similar. "How about 'I Want a Million Dollars for Christmas?' You write a reader letter asking for a million dollars for Christmas. Then I can write a column about the evils of materialism and not worry about offending all the real people writing complaint letters about all of the things that are out of stock, too late to purchase, or too expensive to buy."

Frankie's eyes lit up. "Oohhh... I can totally write that letter. But with the cost of inflation, should it be closer to two million? I really don't know that a million dollars for Christmas would be enough."

"You're right," Tayde agreed. "That's a great idea. Let's calculate the current inflation rate and add it to a million dollars. A weird number will get more attention. You can help me write a ridiculous, fake reader letter. It will essentially be a spoof on the numerous real letters I have received, but this one will be asking for the specific sum of a million dollars plus the cost of inflation. My letter will be to all the materialistic people out there who are overly focused on *things* for Christmas."

Frankie clapped her hands excitedly. "I love it! I think even Sheryl will approve. She likes out-of-the-box stuff. And it will give me a chance to hone my skills in being ridiculous. That's one column. Give me a second column subject, and I'll leave you alone. I don't care about the third column. I'll just play it up as the 'Wright Christmas Eve Column' and sprinkle a little mystery and anticipation."

"No pressure there," Tayde grumbled. She frowned, scrolling again through her email as if hoping one of them would jump out and say, "Pick me!"

Frustrated when she didn't get any enthusiastic volunteers, she leaned back in her chair and extended her hand to gesture at the screen. "It just feels wrong to complain about Christmas, but my inbox is full. Obviously, others don't share my feelings on the subject."

"Maybe you should write that. Talk about how people need to stop complaining. If they see something wrong, they should get off their bums and work to fix it themselves instead of sending an anonymous email to you. If you want to complain about something, own it, show your face, and work to fix it."

"I'm sure a 'get off your bums' Christmas letter will be received well. It's pretty much insulting my own column. The premise of *Wrongs Made Wright* involves allowing readers to complain about something that matters to them and my taking up the cause. It's counterproductive to advocate that they need to be quiet or act on the cause themselves."

"Maybe that's exactly what needs to be said," Frankie maintained.

"I somehow don't think Sheryl will go for that."

Frankie shrugged. "She doesn't need to. Just save the 'get off your bums' column for Christmas Eve. You know Sheryl doesn't always inspect your column before publication. She won't even be here on the twenty-third. I hear she's taking off somewhere with her new boyfriend." Frankie leaned forward, lowered her voice, and put her hand next to her mouth as if telling a secret. "Rumor around the water cooler is that she and Russ Devoe are a hot item."

Tayde rolled her eyes. "Frankie, you're ridiculous. I can't publish that kind of column on Christmas Eve. I need something encouraging and uplifting. Something that helps people appreciate the true meaning of Christmas and helps them enjoy it more fully."

Frankie crinkled her nose distastefully. "If you say so. Maybe I'll talk to Bells about it. I bet he could tell people to get off their Christmas bums for the goodwill of all men and peace on earth."

Tayde's mouth fell open in shock. Then she saw the teasing in Frankie's eyes. She was goading her into a reaction. Tayde laughed. "You do that. But I'm not giving you his number. Find him yourself. Then you can tell me who he is."

"I guess that can be our backup plan, but since you won't go for it, we still need an idea for you. Let me see your inbox. I'll do eeny, meeny, miny, moe and find your letter to respond to."

"Believe it or not, I've tried." Tayde looked around nervously. The first shift had already left for lunch, which meant the office was empty of all but a few people. With Sheryl off-site today, it should be safe. "Come look at this, Frankie. This is the reason I can't focus."

She moved aside so Frankie could sit in her office chair and view the email on her computer screen.

Tayde waited impatiently while Frankie read.

"What do you think, Frankie?" Tayde asked quietly, even

before Frankie had finished.

Frankie turned deliberately away from the screen and looked at Tayde directly, all trace of teasing gone. "I think you'd better leave it alone."

"But what if there's something there? What if he's right and the accepted truth really isn't the truth?"

"Nothing you can do about it. Not your truth." Frankie wasn't usually serious. But she was now.

"I don't think I can let it go," Tayde said honestly. "Maybe I could if I knew for sure that he's just a crackpot. I need to know who this guy is. Can you trace the email?"

Frankie looked at her, an eyebrow raised disapprovingly. "Can I, or will I?"

"Both."

"I'll see what I can do. Against my better judgment."

"Thank you, Frankie."

"Don't thank me. We just made a deal. Pay me by giving me another title for a Christmas column. We'll trade information. No title, no deal."

Frankie retreated to her own cubicle, and Tayde sat back down in her chair. With Frankie on the job, she determined to "get off her bum" and finally get something done.

"Is Frankie coming over tonight?" Knox asked, settling on the couch beside Tayde and picking up the TV remote.

"No. She had a date," Tayde said distractedly.

"A date?" Knox echoed, sounding slightly confused. He stood and walked over to the refrigerator.

Tayde heard the refrigerator door open.

About ten seconds later, it shut, and Knox wandered back to flop down on the couch empty-handed. "You want to watch a movie?" he asked.

"No. Trying to work," Tayde replied, not even shifting her focus from the laptop perched on her lap.

Knox was quiet for about thirty seconds before speaking again. "Did Frankie say who she was going out with?"

Tayde grabbed her phone and handed it to him. "Read her texts yourself."

She already knew that Frankie didn't mention the identity of her date. She'd just reported that the email she'd tried to trace was rerouted through a proxy, so she couldn't identify the original IP address. Then she'd stated that she had a date this evening, but she asked Tayde to keep her end of the bargain and send a title for her Christmas column.

Tayde had quipped back that Frankie hadn't provided any information. Therefore, the deal was null and void.

Frankie hadn't responded, which told Tayde she really was busy.

Knox set the phone on the coffee table and sat back with his arms folded and a sour look on his face. It was rather amusing to see him so bothered.

"What's wrong, Knox?" Tayde asked. "The serial dater can't handle it if someone else has a date and he doesn't?"

"What was she talking about?" Knox asked, ignoring her question. "What email was she trying to trace?"

Knox needed a distraction, or he would drive her nuts and keep her from getting any work done. Tayde brought up the email in question and handed her laptop over to him. Wearily, she stretched her legs out, deciding she needed a break anyway.

"What are you going to do?" Knox asked, finishing the email

and handing the laptop back to her.

"Nothing, I guess. Frankie couldn't find any information on the identity of the sender. Probably just a disgruntled employee. Frankie said I should just let it go." When faced with a dead end, Tayde didn't see that she had much choice.

"I disagree." Knox sat up straight and faced her. His normally teasing gaze was serious. "You're smart, Tayde. You don't need anyone's help. Research it yourself and find out if it's legit."

Tayde shook her head skeptically. "There's no way Sheryl would let me."

"You don't need her permission. Do it on your own time. Just because you look into it doesn't mean you need to write a column about it."

"Then why look into it?" she asked dully. It didn't make sense to do what Knox was proposing. It wasn't logical and presented way too much risk, but part of her eagerly listened to his words.

"Because there is a story there," Knox said, his tone animated. "I'm not saying there's any truth to this person's accusations, but there is a perspective. Someone doesn't have to be right to have a perspective."

Tayde frowned, playing the devil's advocate against what her heart actually believed. "It's probably just sour grapes. Someone got fired and is mad because he blames someone else."

"Maybe."

Knox fell silent, and Tayde wasn't sure if he had anything else to say. Then his words came again, this time in a thoughtful tone. "Do you know why Britany cheated on me? She said she always felt I was too good for her. Not good in the sense of value, but good in the righteous sense. She said she never felt like herself. She was always trying to play the part of the good Christian wife and do the right thing. But it wasn't who she was. She met a guy she felt like herself with. She didn't feel like she had to measure up. She could be herself, and she liked that freedom. I made her feel trapped."

Tayde's heart went out to her brother. "Knox, that's no excuse. You did nothing wrong. She cheated on you!"

Knox nodded, his expression resembling that of a little boy. "I know that. I'm not excusing her behavior. Not saying she was right. She wasn't. But she had a perspective, and that perspective contributed to her choices. Understanding someone's perspective and why they act the way they do is valuable. You aren't required to agree with their choices, but you can still feel a measure of empathy. I feel bad that she felt that way. I feel bad that she turned to someone else's arms for comfort. I'm still very hurt. But I understand a little of the why, and sometimes that helps."

"I still think she's a terrible person," Tayde said flatly. She'd never liked Britany. And sometimes, forgiving someone who'd wronged you was easier than forgiving someone who'd wronged someone you loved.

"I don't think her perspective would earn any tears of sympathy," Knox admitted. "You definitely wouldn't defend her behavior in one of your columns. And you shouldn't." Knox turned serious eyes to Tayde and met her gaze directly. "Whether or not the guy who wrote the letter is right, he has a perspective. And it's probably valuable enough to understand, even if you can't agree."

"It might just be a waste of time." Tayde's voice threaded with fear and uncertainty

Knox shrugged. "Might be. But there's only one way to know for sure."

"I'll think about it," Tayde granted reluctantly. "Let's watch a movie. Something where the good guys are good, the bad guys are bad, and there is no other perspective."

Knox laughed. "I thought you had work."

"I do, but I can't have you moping around because Frankie isn't here to entertain you and feed you dessert!"

Knox chose an action movie, and Tayde was thoroughly satisfied when the hero beat the villain. The ending credits rolled, and Tayde looked over to see Knox curled up asleep on the couch. She shut off the TV and waited, not in a hurry to wake him and send him to bed.

She loved her brother. She would have given anything to keep him from being hurt. He still wasn't fully recovered from Britany, but it was a good sign that he'd talked about her. He'd always avoided conversations about his feelings and any mention of his ex-wife. Yet tonight, he'd volunteered, giving a glimpse of his anguish but also his strength.

For the first time in a long time, Tayde thought he might eventually be okay. And maybe Tayde would eventually be able to forgive Britany herself.

Tayde thought back over what Knox had said, her mouth puckering in a frown. She still wasn't sure what to do about the email.

She picked up her phone and meandered through her texts. She'd texted Bells a few times since last Saturday. It wasn't serious, and he didn't seem to hold a grudge. But she hadn't managed to bring the topic up. Now she thought about calling him. He was the king of perspective. Maybe he could advise her on whether to pursue the letter. But she was afraid to talk to him. She might put her foot in her mouth and say the wrong thing. Despite what he'd said, she felt like she was better in print. Maybe she could express herself better with a text.

Tayde: Need your opinion. What if no perspective gives adequate justification for the wrong committed? What if there had been no good story behind the graveyard baseball? What if the homecoming girl was actually a rude jerk? What if the RV mom abused her kids? What if the boy who threw the chair hadn't been provoked? What if someone's perspective is entirely based on a lie?

The three little lines blinked for several minutes, and Tayde watched every single flash until words appeared on her screen.

Mr. Bells: People don't usually do wrong things intentionally. They don't wake up each morning thinking they'll make bad choices that day. People screw up. Sin is real. People usually do what they think is best in an individual moment. Even if they are wrong, even if you can't agree, there's still value in perspectives different from your own.

Tayde: So even if there's no factual truth, a perspective might still hold value without it?

Mr. Bells: Tayde Wright, you want to right wrongs and make a difference. We can't make the world a better place unless we see ourselves in the face of others, especially those who are different from us.

It's the same thing Knox had said, which made Tayde wonder exactly how much Knox and Bells had talked lately.

You don't have to agree to empathize with someone's circumstances.

The thought floated through her head. She wondered about the person who wrote the email and the circumstances that had prompted him to do so. If she pursued this story, it may cost her her job. But what if this person needed a voice, just like the boy with anger issues? What if God had put this letter in her path because He wanted her to be that voice?

Ok, Lord. I'll do it! I need a Christmas story. I can't get this one out of my head. I don't have any illusions about my abilities. Instead, help me stumble over the truth. And if there's a story that needs to be told, help me to find the courage to tell it.

Chapter Sixteen

Tayde pulled up in front of the modest, single-story house and shut off the car's engine. Was she really doing this? She'd spent the last week researching an event that had happened fifteen years ago. She'd read every news mention, combed through court notes and documents, and internet stalked all the people involved until she knew the color of their eyes and their favorite restaurants. Everything Tayde found confirmed the official story that Jeff Bennett had been solely responsible for swindling numerous people out of millions of dollars under the guise of bookkeeper for Devonce Investments. The evidence against him was solid and irrefutable.

It appeared there was absolutely nothing to the mysterious email Tayde had received.

But Tayde still couldn't let it go.

Tomorrow was Christmas Eve. She already had a column

written to post. It was sweet, encouraging, and completely meaningless. It wouldn't stay with the reader longer than a passing smile. But she could be done. She didn't have to be here. She'd completed her tasks and could go home and enjoy the holiday and a few days off work.

But then she'd never know.

She'd been extremely cautious with her research. She couldn't actually talk to anyone for fear word would get back to Sheryl or Russ Devoe. Anyone connected to the fraud case was also connected to them, and asking questions about a closed case would surely get her fired.

She reasoned that the only person she could talk to was the one convicted of the crime. But Jeff Bennett had died in prison about five years after he was sentenced. Tayde had read his obituary. It was brief, just a small notification stating that Jeff Bennett was survived by his two children. His son was listed as a resident of California. But his daughter—Maya Bennett Sandoval—was listed as hailing from Brighton Falls.

Tayde found the daughter's current address and couldn't shake the urge to go see her. She'd been fifteen at the time of her father's arrest. She may not have any actual facts, but she may have a perspective about what had happened. And she was unlikely to contact Sheryl or Russ and tattle on Tayde.

Tayde took a deep breath and stepped out of the car. She'd have a five-minute conversation, and that would be enough to quiet her preoccupation with this story. Then Tayde would go home, kick off her shoes, and send off her other column to be published.

Tayde walked to the front door and knocked.

A pretty woman about Tayde's age opened the door with a baby on her hip. Based on her social media stalking, Tayde recognized her as Maya Sandoval.

Tayde hurried to get it all said before she lost her nerve. "Hi! I'm Tayde Wright. I'm sorry. I should have called ahead. I just wasn't sure I'd actually come. I was wondering if you could answer a couple of questions about what happened with your father fifteen years ago."

Maya's eyes immediately became guarded and suspicious. "Are you like a reporter? I've told other TV shows that I'm not interested."

"I am a reporter. But not that kind." Tayde paused, struggling to explain. If Maya thought she was out to humiliate her father further by reaffirming her father's guilt in a documentary of some kind, she'd never speak to Tayde. Finally, Tayde spread her hands wide and said honestly, "I write a column for a magazine. I received a reader letter indicating that the story fed to the public of what happened fifteen years ago with Devonce Investments may not have been the complete truth. I was interested in hearing your perspective on what happened."

Maya gave a brief nod and opened the door wide. "Come in." She led the way to a small living room and indicated Tayde was welcome to sit. A little girl, who looked to be about three years old, sat on the floor playing with some blocks. Maya perched on a chair and held the baby in her lap.

Tayde looked around at the modest home. Maya obviously wasn't wealthy, but the small home was clean and cluttered with toys. Her children were chubby and full of shy smiles. Maya was obviously a loving mother, and everything about her said she was someone whose word Tayde could trust.

"In fifteen years, nobody has ever asked me about my perspective," Maya said slowly. "They usually ask questions to try to make my dad look pure evil. Nobody has ever bothered to come looking for the truth."

"And what is the truth?" Tayde asked gently.

Maya looked at her and replied unflinchingly, "Oh, my dad was guilty. He participated in the fraud. But that's the black-and-white truth. People never ask why he did it. They just assumed it was greed."

"But it wasn't?" Tayde asked breathlessly.

"No. It was love. My dad did it to try to save my mom. Dad started working for Devonce right before my mom was diagnosed with cancer. I think Devoe started asking Dad to do illegal things, and Dad couldn't say no because Mom's treatment depended on his insurance and income." As she spoke, Maya bounced the happy baby on her knee.

"But that implicates Russ Devoe." Tayde couldn't just assume. If Maya's words were true, that changed the entire story on which her father's conviction had rested.

Maya scoffed. "Of course it does! If a rational person looked at Devoe's lifestyle fifteen years ago and compared it to my dad's, it would be obvious Dad wasn't the guy reaping the benefits of the fraud."

"But all of the evidence said that Jeff Bennett acted alone." Tayde didn't want to offend Maya so much that she stopped talking, but she had to know. And so far, Maya seemed like a strong woman.

"Dad was a convenient scapegoat," Maya said flatly. Then she cast a glance at her busy three-year-old across the room. She slipped down to the floor and placed the baby right in front of her outstretched legs. She spread a few toys out in front of him.

Then she leaned forward to Tayde and lowered her voice. "The woman who wrote that exposé was Russ Devoe's girlfriend. She was sleeping with him. So, they framed my dad, but it wasn't hard. He was already guilty. They just concocted a bit more evidence so all the blame shifted squarely on his shoulders."

"But there must have been some evidence," Tayde said, following suit and lowering her voice to match Maya's. "Your dad didn't even fight it. He accepted a plea deal, which wasn't even a good deal! He got ten years in prison!"

Maya lifted her shoulders and let them drop helplessly. A sad smile played about her lips. "My mom got sick again. Somehow, the money for her treatment magically showed up. We never paid for a single medical bill, our mortgage was paid on time every month, and we had groceries delivered free of charge."

Tayde's voice came in a shocked whisper. "Are you saying your dad was paid to take the fall?"

Maya leaned forward even more, her eyes intense. "I'm saying that every time there was a school dance, a dress magically appeared on my doorstep. Jeff Bennett wasn't paid in cash, but his family was taken care of. And that was the only hope he had to save my mom."

"But even that didn't work," Tayde paused. So far, Maya had kept tight control of her emotions, providing an excellent, concise testimony. "I read her obituary." She met Maya's gaze with sympathy.

Maya's eyes filled with tears, and she nodded. "She lived a little over a year after Dad was sent to prison. She hung on until my brother turned eighteen. I was fifteen, but I was allowed to stay with him as my official guardian. We used the life insurance money to pay off the house. But after she died, the magical money stopped. Since that day, my brother and I have worked for every little thing we have."

"If the money stopped, why didn't your dad appeal and get a new trial?" The injustice of it made Tayde shift uncomfortably in her chair.

Maya flashed that same sad smile. "It's really hard to appeal a plea bargain and an admission of guilt." She held a toy and shook it for the baby, the merry sound contrasting the hopelessness her words conveyed. "My brother tried. My dad was completely defeated after Mom died and wouldn't even try. The public defender wouldn't even speak to us. My brother worked his way through college and became a lawyer because of it. But my dad passed away during his first year of law school."

Tayde was quiet, thinking.

The little girl came and sat on her mom's lap for a snuggle, which immediately made the baby jealous. He awkwardly tried to insert himself between his mom and his sister, babbling the whole time.

Maya laughed at them and put one child on each side of her lap. Then she looked up at Tayde. Though her expression contained shadows of sadness, she had not let her family's tragedy define her. "Thank you for coming and asking for my perspective. It was nice to feel heard, even if it won't do any good. I think I've done okay for myself. I got married young, but I made it through college. I'm an interior designer. We have three children. My oldest is in kindergarten." She shrugged and held her babies close. "Sometimes bad things happen in life, and there's nothing you can do about it. Life is rarely fair. Nobody cares what happened fifteen years ago to a man who is no longer present on earth."

"I care," Tayde insisted. "It isn't right. People should know the truth of what happened."

Maya's kids crawled off her lap and started chasing each other around the room. It was a slow-motion chase, however. The baby would set off crawling, trying to reach his sister. She'd let him get close and then squeal and take off on all fours crawling away from him. The baby would giggle and start after her again.

Maya smiled as she watched her kids but told Tayde quietly, "You know it won't do any good. It's all hearsay. Even if you had evidence, it would be pointless. The statute of limitations on fraud has long passed. There's no way to prove that Devoe paid for our expenses and Mom's cancer treatment in exchange for Dad taking the fall. Devoe got away with it, and there is nothing you or I can do about it."

Something in Tayde rebelled at Maya's words. "'Speak up for those who cannot speak for themselves, for the rights of all who are destitute,'" Tayde quoted. The words of Proverbs 31:8 had echoed through Tayde's mind since she'd come across it earlier that week. She knew she was at a crossroads. If she accepted that it was pointless to do anything, that verse would haunt her.

She held Maya's gaze steadily and spoke her thoughts as they formed. "Your father can no longer speak for himself. Maybe I should say something because it's right, even if I cannot see any earthly good for doing so."

Maya stood, picked up the baby, and placed him in Tayde's lap. "Wait here." She disappeared from the room, leaving Tayde and the little boy to eye each other. His big, blue eyes inspected Tayde, and she felt the weight of an old soul behind them. It was as if he were watching her, waiting to see if she would follow through on the big words she'd just proclaimed.

Maya reappeared and traded Tayde a book for the baby. "This is my mother's last journal. You should probably read my dad's story if you intend to tell it. Mom always kept a journal of thoughts and prayers. She never finished that one. The last entry is a few days before she passed."

"What does she say?" Tayde asked, inspecting the volume almost reverently.

Maya bit her lip, gazing at the journal with a touch of anxiety. "I don't really know. I've never been brave enough emotionally to read it. My brother has, though. My dad always got Mom a journal for her birthday in November. This journal was the last one. He was arrested on Christmas Eve. She died a little over a year later. If you're interested in perspectives, this tells hers."

"Thank you," Tayde said, awed that Maya was entrusting such an irreplaceable treasure to her. "I will read it and return it to you."

Maya nodded. "You should probably also talk to my brother. He read that journal and researched a lot before my dad's passing. Let me write down his contact information for you."

Maya walked over to the counter and wrote on a sticky note.

"Thank you," Tayde said gratefully. She wouldn't turn down any possible lead, but she hurried to explain, "I don't know if I will have time to contact him. I read in your dad's obituary that he lives in California. That's why I contacted you."

"He lives here in Brighton Falls now," Maya said, handing Tayde the sticky note. "He was living in California and attending law school when Dad passed. But he came back after he graduated."

Tayde accepted the note and flipped open the journal's cover to safely attach it. "Thanks. I'd love to talk to him, but I'm in a time crunch. If I write this story, it will be tonight. And it will be published tomorrow."

Maya's eyes widened.

Tayde smiled. "I work for a magazine now owned by Devoe. My boss is Sheryl Sutton. She won't review my column scheduled to release on Christmas Eve. It's my only chance."

Maya blinked in shock. "But if you write anything implicating them, you will lose your job."

"Yes, I will," Tayde said firmly. "I've been thinking about writing a letter of resignation and sending it at the same time the column posts."

Maya gasped. "I just realized who you are! I've read your column—*Wrongs Made Wright!*"

Tayde walked to the door. "If you've read my column, you can probably guess that my biggest fear is not losing my job but that Mr. Bells will add his two cents into the mix."

"You speak. I'll pray." The words came simply and quietly, catching Tayde's attention. She swung back around, taking in the fifteen years of hope reflected in Maya's eyes.

Instead of feeling daunted, determination filled her veins. With Maya praying, maybe she really could speak.

Dear World,

What if it is too late to right a wrong?

A letter found my eyes fifteen years too late. The statute of limitations on any crime had passed. The accusation included my boss and the company I work for. The claims differed entirely from the solid story accepted by law enforcement and the public alike. The case was closed.

It didn't make sense to take any action other than pushing the delete button.

But it bothered me.

Mr. Bells has pointed out so often the mystery behind perspective, and I was fascinated by this one. Even if I investigated and found out the perspective wasn't based on facts, could it still be valuable? Maybe the thoughts, feelings, and motivations carry an intrinsic value greater than any right or wrong with them.

In my investigation, I discovered that a man named Jeff Bennett was arrested in front of his teenage children on this exact day—Christmas Eve—fifteen years ago. The widely accepted "facts" proclaimed that Bennett was solely responsible for a large-scale Ponzi scheme with his role as the bookkeeper for Devonce Investments. Owner and CEO Russ Devoe was cleared of wrongdoing along with everyone else. Bennett signed a confession and took a plea deal that included a ten-year prison sentence. The case was closed. Life moved on. A little over a year later, Bennett's wife, Patricia, passed away after a long battle with cancer. Five years into his prison sentence, Jeff Bennett also passed away.

Instead of relating a different perspective on this story, I thought I'd let Jeff Bennett tell you himself. The following is a letter Bennett sent to his wife shortly after beginning his prison sentence.

My love,

I need you to know the truth. The rest of the world can believe the worst of me as long as you and the kids know I am not the horrible monster they claim. I am guilty of fraud. I participated knowing it was fraud, but I did it on Russ Devoe's instructions. If I did what he said, I kept my job and insurance to cover the cost of your medical care. I tried to back out, but by then, he threatened to frame me for everything and pointed out that you would not receive the care you needed to fight the return of cancer.

In the end, he framed me anyway. In keeping the books and managing the money, I was fully aware of what was going on. But I did not do everything they claimed.

I've had a lot of time to think. I realized that Russ has planned this for a while. Sheryl was careful not to implicate him in her article, and they both had all the evidence against me ready for when her story was released. I think Devonce was already being investigated. Sheryl's story was a plan to get him out of the mess while launching her career. Russ's closest friends pulled their money out the day before the story dropped. I did the transactions myself. All of the company's cash was distributed before assets were frozen. Devoe knew what was about to happen, and he and his friends escaped with as much money as possible. Money I'm sure they will reinvest in rebuilding the company now that they've divorced the "guilty party."

But all of this is for your eyes only. I can't breathe a word of the truth, nor can you. Russ made me a deal. He will pay for everything if I accept the sole blame for the fraud. You won't pay anything for the clinical trial or any other experimental treatment needed. He will cover the cost of our mortgage, food, and anything the kids need. It will be done anonymously, but you won't need to worry. You and the kids will be taken care of.

No, I don't trust him, but I've hidden evidence that can implicate him. If he doesn't keep his end of the bargain, I will tell you where to find my files, and he will go to jail. Russ's guilt doesn't change mine. I'd still do prison time and not be able to care for you. This is the only way to support you and the kids. This is my only hope of saving your life, so you're there to meet me when this nightmare is over.

I hate the shame I have brought on you. I can't lose you. I know it was wrong. But to me, the greater sin would be not doing everything possible to save you. May God and my beloved Patricia forgive me.

Love,
Jeff

Patricia Bennett kept the letter in her journal, which was shown to me by their daughter. I also found a picture of Jeff and Patricia Bennett posing with another couple within its pages. The couple, with arms around each other, is clearly recognizable as Sheryl Sutton and Russ Devoe. Upon further inspection of the volume, I found something inserted into its spine. It was a flash drive full of intact files detailing every transaction Bennett made, along with the evidence showing the instructions came from Devoe. Just like Jeff had told his wife, he had hidden evidence for her to find if needed.

Patricia Bennett passed away a year after her husband was arrested. Jeff Bennett passed away in prison five years later. It's too late for exoneration.

Any crimes committed fifteen years ago cannot be charged. It's too late for justice.

In many ways, it is too late to right this wrong.

But it isn't too late to be a voice.

Many centuries ago, I'm sure people felt like it was too late to right a wrong. The sin of the world was too much. It had gone on too long. Promises had seemingly gone unanswered. It was too late.

Then a baby was born in a stable in Bethlehem, destined to right the wrongs no one else could.

Instead of late, He was right on time.

I'm sending this out into the world, into the hands of all who read it to do with it what you can, trusting that it's right on time too.

I think I can hear the bells.

Tayde Wright

Chapter Seventeen

"It's published," Frankie whispered.

At the soft announcement, Tayde pushed the button to send her resignation letter.

"Let's get out of here," Tayde said with a shiver. Even though they were the office's only occupants, whispering felt appropriate.

"It's about time." Frankie turned off the computer and stood. They'd been up all night. Frankie had stayed at Tayde's side the whole time, helping her pound out the column and acting in the role of editor.

They'd finally finished in the early hours of the morning. Frankie couldn't post the column remotely, so they'd snuck into the office to finish the job. Technically, it wasn't sneaking. Frankie had a key, but when you were publishing a column that essentially set fire to the building, it sure felt like sneaking.

They'd only turned one light on in the room, making the task feel even more clandestine. Now that it was done, neither one of them wanted to be here.

"Sheryl is going to know you helped me," Tayde worried.

"I'm not sending her my resignation," Frankie said indignantly. "I want her to look me in the eye when she fires me. Let's see if she can hold her head up when she realizes everyone knows she is a complete fake. Her claim to fame is a bunch of lies to cover for the thief she was sleeping with."

"You go ahead. I never want to see her again." Strangely, Tayde didn't feel one bit of regret about quitting. She felt relief. No longer would she need to write what someone else wanted her to. Even without posting her bombshell of a column, Tayde realized she was done with Chronicle and everything Sheryl wanted it to be. "I just feel bad for her son and her grandson. And her cat. She's not the person I thought she was."

"Everyone is a mixture of good and bad," Frankie said insightfully. "I don't think Russ and Sheryl are pure evil. Big mistakes usually result from a hundred small missteps and bad decisions. They did some awful things, and they should pay for their actions, but that doesn't mean Sheryl doesn't love her son and grandson very much. There's probably at least a little gray in her black heart."

"How did you get to be so wise?" Tayde asked, looking at her quirky friend in surprise.

She frowned dramatically. "I know this advice columnist and her lovable nemesis who keep harping on believing the best of others and seeing different perspectives. Besides, have you considered that there may be a mastermind behind it all? Maybe Sheryl and Russ are just pawns. I honestly think it's the cat who runs everything. Have you met the cat?"

Tayde laughed at Frankie's wide-eyed, dramatic expression.

Yes, she had met the cat!

Frankie glanced at the clock, and the fun suddenly drained from her face. "Come on!" Frankie urged. "We need to get out of here!"

Frankie was right. They didn't want to be here if Sheryl or Russ showed up. Tayde reached down to grab Patricia Bennet's journal from where she'd set it on the desk. The front cover caught on her finger and came open. Tayde's eyes fell on the sticky note she'd put there yesterday.

Suddenly, she started choking on her own air.

"What's wrong?" Frankie's cry came frantic as she looked around, trying to figure out what was killing her friend.

"It's him!" Tayde pointed to the innocent blue square of paper.

"Who?" Frankie asked, still clueless.

"Bells! It's Bells!" Tayde said, still pointing as if the paper were a gigantic spider.

Frankie picked it up. "Gavin Bennett? Who is he?"

Tayde took a deep breath, trying to formulate her chaotic thoughts into words. "He's Jeff and Patricia Bennett's son. Maya's older brother. And he's Mr. Bells!"

Frankie looked at the paper as if it held a hidden clue. "How do you know?"

Tayde grabbed her phone and brought up the contact for Mr. Bells. "I recognized the phone number. It's *his* phone number. They match. When the only real information you have about someone is his phone number, you know it. I've googled it, studied it, and called phone companies. I know his number better than my own."

Tayde flashed her phone screen in front of Frankie's face and pointed to the exact match on the blue post-it note. There was no maybe.

Frankie sat back down on the office chair. "So, all this time...?"

Tayde opened the browser on her phone and typed in "Gavin Bennett, Brighton Falls." Sure enough, a law firm came up with Gavin Bennett listed as an employee. She clicked the "Meet the Team" button. A picture of a handsome man, along with a short bio, filled the screen.

Frankie crowded behind Tayde, looking at the screen. "Wow, he's nice to look at."

Tayde read quickly. "He was an English major for his undergrad," she moaned. "Maya said he became a lawyer because of what happened to their dad."

"It looks like he does a lot of pro bono work and public defending," Frankie summarized. "Just think what an amazing coincidence it is! The story you stumbled on was Mr. Bells' own story!"

Tayde shut her eyes against the pain as the truth came close and suffocating. "It's not a coincidence, Frankie. It was his plan. He wrote the reader letter that started me investigating."

"Really?" Frankie said doubtfully. "You think so?"

"I know so. He's been playing me this whole time. He wanted me to clear his dad's name. He used me, and I played right into his hand."

"I guess that explains why he kept responding but never told you who he was." Frankie took the phone from Tayde and zoomed in on Gavin's handsome face. "Too bad. He seems like a nice guy."

"He was leading me down the road like a dog on a leash," Tayde seethed. The more she thought about it, the angrier she became.

"What will you do? Frankie asked. "It's too late to pull the column. With the ads I made, it's probably made it around the world twice by now."

Tayde blinked in surprise. "I didn't know you ran ads for it."

"Just the usual. Needed to give a little microphone to a deserving story." Frankie didn't seem to share Tayde's righteous anger directed toward Gavin Bennett. Instead, her words were threaded with compassion for her friend. "You did a good thing, Tayde. Even if Gavin was shady in getting it done, it was still the right thing to do, and the way you presented it was beautiful."

"I don't regret the column, but I don't intend to let Gavin off easily." Resolve replaced Tayde's shock and hurt. "Mr. Bells told me to find him, so that's exactly what I intend to do."

She picked up the journal once more and headed out of the office with determination. She flipped off the light switch as she passed, returning the room to darkness.

"Tayde, you're on your own for this one," Frankie said, hurrying to catch up. "It's Christmas Eve, and I haven't slept at all. I need to get a few hours of shuteye before tonight. I have plans."

"That's fine," Tayde waved her off. "I'll go on my own."

She stepped aside for Frankie to follow her through the front door.

Frankie shot a worried glance in her direction. "Come to think of it, maybe you should get some sleep before you track this guy down. You don't know where to find him."

"Oh, I know where to find him," Tayde assured. "The law firm advertised that they were open until noon on Christmas Eve."

"Really?" Frankie was not pleased. "What kind of law firm is open on Christmas Eve?"

"The kind that is wrapping gifts to deliver to the children of inmates," Tayde mumbled. "They said that on the website too."

Frankie gasped dramatically. "Those stinkin' do-gooders!"

Tayde pulled open her car door, but Frankie stepped in front of her. "Tayde, please. Just go home and get some sleep. I'm not saying you're not thinking clearly now. But you're running on fumes. You haven't slept in over twenty-four hours. You might think differently after a little sleep."

"I'm fine, Frankie," Tayde assured, gently pushing her away. "I couldn't sleep now anyway. Not until I finish this."

Frankie reluctantly stepped aside. Tayde got into her car and checked the law firm's address on her phone.

She didn't allow herself to think. Thinking hurt too badly. She didn't have a plan for when she got there. She just drove.

She pulled into the parking lot and walked to the front door. It certainly wasn't a fancy law firm. It was a single one-story building in an older part of town. She stepped inside, noting that the interior was tastefully decorated and inviting, but it wasn't extravagant. The floor was done in a laminate that resembled tile. Gray chairs clustered in a waiting room area. Decorative plants interspersed the open space, and beautiful landscapes adorned the wall. It wasn't the typical law office décor, but Tayde liked it, though reluctantly. She idly wondered if Maya had been the interior designer.

She walked straight over to a woman who sat behind a counter. "Mr. Bells, please," she announced simply.

Confusion clouded the young woman's face. "There's no one here by that name."

Tayde could hear laughter and conversation emanating from another room. "Can you please just go tell them that Tayde Wright is requesting to see Mr. Bells?"

The receptionist looked at Tayde like she was unstable, and maybe that's the reason she complied, walking with heels clicking to where she disappeared down a hallway.

Tayde heard the sound from the other room pause. The receptionist returned, followed by a tall man in a suit. Tayde recognized him by his picture on the website.

His eyes collided with hers, instantly shooting her heart off like a rocket.

"Hi, Tayde."

The warm, soothing voice was familiar. She didn't know what she expected him to say, but it wasn't that. He wasn't surprised. It was almost as if he'd been expecting her. He'd casually just said two words, and she was already unnerved.

Before she could force any words out, Gavin inclined his head to the side and said, "We can talk in my office."

Tayde followed him. As they turned down a hallway, she saw several faces leaning out from a door, comical in their curious observation. Gavin opened another door and waved to the curious faces before entering.

"Feel free to leave the door open if you want," Gavin said. "Just know that my coworkers will eagerly hang on your every word."

Tayde shut the door firmly.

She turned back, determined to take control of the conversation. But his gaze immediately caught hers and held. She knew those honest blue eyes. She'd studied them before. If she wasn't careful, she would become lost in them again, exactly as she had the night of the gala.

"I read the column," his words came quietly. "It was beautifully written. Thank you."

Tayde blinked, suddenly finding her voice. "That's all you have to say? 'Thank you'? You manipulated me from the beginning. It was all a set-up."

For the first time, Gavin looked shocked. "No, Tayde. It wasn't like that at all."

"You sent a fake letter to me, Gavin," Tayde threw out. "I talked to you after that. I even asked your advice. But you never mentioned, 'Hey, Tayde, that was me.'"

Anger flashed in Gavin's eyes. "You wrote a fake letter too. You did it to write a story you thought needed to be told. I did the same thing."

"Writing an anonymous story is different than deliberately deceiving me," Tayde gritted out. "This whole time, you've been using me."

"No, I haven't." Gavin's eyes were wide and honest. "I didn't plan this. I didn't intend for any of this to happen. I saw an opportunity to right a wrong, and I took it."

He was a liar. She couldn't trust him. He looked so perfect standing there like the cover of a magazine. His suit was perfectly pressed. Not even a strand of hair dared to deviate from its assigned place. Even the backdrop of his office was picture-perfect. Unlike the traditional rich, dark lawyer's office, Gavin's was light and airy. Natural light from the window illuminated the plants and white furnishings with blue accents.

"If that's all it was, why didn't you just tell me who you were?" she demanded.

He readily responded, "Because then you wouldn't have investigated Jeff Bennett. I knew you would find me all on your own."

"And I did find you." Tayde stepped forward, catching a glimpse of a picture on his desk. It was a picture of Maya and her kids. "I found out exactly what kind of man you are. It's all a sham. All of your holier-than-thou words, every time you wrote as Mr. Bells, every text, every conversation, the meeting at the gala, even your nice guy persona—it was all part of a genius plan to get me to redeem your dad's name."

"You really think that's all it was? Just an elaborate

scheme?" Gavin looked at her incredulously. "You think too much of my intelligence. I'm no Machiavelli, neither in genius nor insanity. After everything you just mentioned, I would have thought you knew me better."

"I don't believe a word you say," Tayde whispered. "You got what you wanted. Your dad's story was published, and his reputation exonerated. Now please leave me alone."

Yet she was the one who'd come to him. And now, she was done.

"Tayde, please," he pleaded, reaching a hand out to her. "Let me explain."

But she didn't want to. She wanted to escape. She might be tempted to take his hand and listen to him if she stayed. Then she might even like his explanation. Then she might melt into those eyes and want him to hold her. She clung to her anger because anything different was just too much.

"I don't want to hear it," she put her hand up to stop any oncoming words. "I don't regret posting the story about your dad. But I regret you. I thought you cared about me. I cared about you. Now that your pawn has successfully completed her mission, you are free to pat yourself on the back for a job well done and walk away from me with a clear conscience."

Tayde turned and reached for the doorknob.

"Tayde, wait! Please stop!" He stepped up behind her, but she'd already made it through the door. He followed, his words imploring, "At least let me explain. You can be mad at me all you want afterward. But let me explain!"

She refused to stop or turn. "Nothing you say will make a difference. You got what you wanted. Goodbye, Mr. Bells."

Tayde walked out of the office, past the ogling coworkers, the nervous receptionist who surely had 911 on speed dial ready to go, the attractive potted plants, and the front door. She got into her car and drove away without a backward glance. She gritted her teeth and refused to think, pushing wave upon wave of emotion away. Anger was the only emotion she allowed herself to feel.

She didn't stop until she made it home, shut her bedroom door, and collapsed on her bed with instant, convulsing sobs.

She hadn't even known the guy. Why did it have to hurt so much that she'd merely been the means to an end?

She curled up on the bed and shut her eyes tightly, desperately hoping for exhaustion to finally whisk her off into the place of nothingness where no one would ever ask her if she could hear the bells.

Chapter Eighteen

"Have I told you how proud I am of you?" Tayde's dad wrapped an arm around her shoulder and gently kissed her hair.

"Not in the last few minutes," Tayde replied, smiling up at him.

It was Christmas morning. Their family tradition was to have breakfast at Tayde's parents' house, just as they'd done when they were little. Tayde's mom always went all out for the occasion. The room was saturated with the delicious smells of bacon, cinnamon rolls, and coffee. After breakfast, they'd gather around the tree for presents. Tayde was helping to set the table while her younger sister, Averie, had locked herself in a bedroom to finish up the gift wrapping she'd procrastinated.

"I don't think I've ever been so proud to have an unemployed daughter." David Wright's eyes sparkled with humor.

"I've gotten several job offers in the last twenty-four hours," Tayde reported. "I shouldn't be unemployed for long."

"Don't decide right away," he cautioned. "Play hard to get. You're soon to be an award-winning author. I'm sure you'll win the Nobel Prize."

"It's the Pulitzer for writing, Dave!" Vickie called from the kitchen. They heard the clanging sound of her pulling a tray of cinnamon rolls out of the oven and setting it on the counter.

Her dad looked off in the distance and raised his hand as if tracing the words on an imaginary billboard. "Tayde Wright, the Nobel Pulitzer winner. I can just see it now."

Tayde smiled at his antics, but they didn't earn an outright laugh. She still felt emotionally drained from yesterday. She'd slept most of the day, finally waking in the evening to find she'd slept through dozens of calls and texts. Friends, coworkers, news reporters, and even the FBI called requesting to speak to her.

She'd returned many of the calls, at least those that had seemed legit. She'd turned down all interview requests, asked for time to consider job offers, and reiterated all the information she knew with the FBI agent. Russ Devoe and Sheryl Sutton couldn't be tried on any fifteen-year-old fraud charges, yet the FBI still seemed very interested in past events. She'd had to meet the agent down at his office so they could take possession of Jeff Bennett's letter, his thumb drive of evidence, and Patricia Bennett's journal. And all that had happened on Christmas Eve.

Tayde's phone beeped with a notification. She looked at the screen and her stomach dropped.

Mr. Bells: Please meet me at the park on the corner of 8th and State St at 12:00. Please let me explain.

After what she'd said to him yesterday, Tayde didn't think he'd ever contact her again. Her fingers hovered over the keypad as she debated how to respond. She could say she was busy with her family. She could say she just wasn't emotionally up to conversation right now. But instead, she kept the reply simple.

Tayde: No.

Tayde's mom appeared from the kitchen, drying her hands worriedly on a towel. "I don't know where your brother is. He's never missed a Christmas breakfast before."

Tayde looked down at her phone again, but she had no messages from Knox and no reply from Gavin. "He didn't mention any—"

The front door opened. Knox stepped in and moved aside for a woman to enter in front of him.

"Frankie!" Tayde exclaimed, hurrying forward for a hug. "I didn't know you were coming!"

Knox nervously cleared his throat. "Mom, Dad, this is my girlfriend, Frankie."

Startled, Tayde's gaze swung from Frankie to Knox and back again. Knox looked slightly uncomfortable, but his arm around Frankie's waist said he was more nervous about his parents than about her. Frankie didn't appear shy or nervous at all and eagerly exchanged greetings.

Vickie fluttered around the couple like an overly excited chicken. "Frankie, we're so glad to have you with us! Everything is ready!"

Breakfast was placed on the table, and everyone sat to enjoy the meal and lively conversation. Frankie fit right in and soon had the whole family almost choking on the food with laughter.

As usual, Tayde's mom urged several extra cinnamon rolls her way and even plopped one on her plate after Tayde refused. Tayde knew she wasn't the only one who hadn't recovered from the trauma of her teenage years. There were subtle signs that it was still there. Even though Tayde was a healthy weight and had been ever since she'd recovered from surgery, her mom was forever stuck trying to make her eat and plump up. If left up to her mom, Tayde would weigh as much as an elephant!

As it was, she understood the situation for what it was and subtly reached over and moved the cinnamon roll from her plate to her brother's. Knox looked down, saw a cinnamon roll, and immediately adopted it and began eating.

As they finished, Tayde's mom announced, "Let's get everything cleaned up. Then presents! Frankie, why don't you help me with the dishes? Knox and Tayde can clear the table."

"I still have some presents to wrap!" Averie announced, hurrying out of the room.

"As usual, Averie's getting out of the work," Knox grumbled.

Frankie followed Vickie, David left to make sure the tree and presents were ready, and Tayde and Knox picked up the dishes.

Knox cast a nervous look into the kitchen, and Tayde knew he was worried about leaving Frankie with his mom and her smothering attention.

"Don't worry," Tayde replied. "Frankie can hold her own. Mom doesn't know what she's in for."

A slow smile stretched Knox's face. "You're right," he said. "Maybe I should worry about Mom!"

"So, when did this happen? And why didn't you tell me?" Tayde asked, tossing a napkin at him playfully.

"You've been pretty busy," Knox said, turning serious. "I was afraid of jinxing it. It was easy to tell you about all the women I dated and never cared about. But Frankie is different.

I'm still afraid to blink and find out she doesn't want anything to do with me."

"I don't think you have to worry about that with Frankie," Tayde assured. "She's had a thing for you for a while."

Knox's eyes widened. "Really? Why didn't you say anything?"

Tayde looked at him with an eyebrow raised. "You've not exactly gone for Frankie's type before. She's too smart and independent. She's not the kind to stroke your ego or stay out all night going to nightclubs. She brings you pie, plays card games, and tells you when you're being an idiot."

Knox's eyes sparkled. "I know. I like it."

"I'm glad you stopped being an idiot long enough to realize it." Tayde took the last of the dishes to the kitchen and grabbed a sponge to clean off the table.

"What about you?" Knox asked. "Have you stopped being an idiot about Mr. Bells?"

"His name is Gavin Bennett," Tayde replied tightly.

"I know. Frankie told me."

"He used me," Tayde said simply, vigorously scrubbing a spot on the table.

"Did he say that?" Knox pressed. "Or is that just what you say?"

Tayde blew out an exasperated breath. "He didn't have to say anything. It was obvious."

Knox leveled an amused look at her and spoke as if trying to extract information from a child. "When you went and talked to him yesterday, did you let him say any actual words, or did you just give him a piece of your mind?"

"I was upset," Tayde said defensively.

Knox shook his head incredulously. "Tayde, you just wrote a life-changing column about valuing another's perspective, even if that person appears guilty as sin. Don't you think you should at least give the guy a chance to tell you his story?"

"Are you calling me a hypocrite, Knox?"

"No. I'm calling you human," he shot back. His tone softened, and he put a gentle hand on her back. "It's difficult to see the world from someone else's point of view, especially when your emotions are involved. But I know a sixteen-year-old girl who would have given anything to have someone see things from her perspective. You try to hide it, but I know what that did to you. I wish I would have believed you so you wouldn't have had to fight alone."

Tayde startled. Knox had never mentioned anything about her struggles as a teen. They'd never spoken of it, and she'd never been sure how much he'd been aware of. His words about perspective hit a mark nothing else could, but the guilt clouding his face bothered her.

She shook her head. "You were a kid, Knox. There's nothing you could have done."

"Maybe not. But it still bothers me." He fell silent, lost in thought. But then the words began flowing in an unexpected confession. "I remember all the times I tattled on you for not eating your food. I remember complaining when you didn't do chores because you said you were too sick. I saw you curled up in pain and thought you were faking it. I was scared of what would happen because of what Mom and Dad said. I was relieved when they left you at the facility. It may not have changed what happened, but I could have been compassionate, listened, and believed you."

Tayde stepped forward and put her arms around her brother, leaning her head against his chest. She willed her love to transfer through her arms to him so he'd know there was nothing to forgive. "It was a long time ago, Knox. I'm fine. I don't hold any resentment against you or anyone else."

Knox hugged her back and affectionately rested his chin on her head. "I know that. But I still think about it, and I hope I always do. Because of it, I've always tried to give people the benefit of the doubt. It hit me hard when I realized I'd failed to investigate the perspective of my student who threw the chair. It brought up a lot of memories of what happened to you."

Knox pulled back and tried to catch her eye as he said gently, "Tayde, I don't want you to hurt someone else the way you were hurt."

Tayde couldn't look at him. Her eyes burned as she fought to hold back tears.

"Why don't you just text him?" Knox said gently. "Give him a chance to explain. You don't have to believe him. But you should let him speak."

Tayde shook her head. She understood what Knox was saying. She just couldn't conjure up the strength to do what he asked. "I just can't today, Knox. He lied to me. Maybe I'll try in a few days."

"But it's Christmas, Tayde," he pressed, reaching out to squeeze her hand. "What if he's hurting just as much as you are?"

Tayde didn't know how to respond, so she didn't. Her mom and Frankie came from the kitchen, and Averie emerged from her hideout with her arms full of wrapped presents.

Knox smiled at Frankie, and with his attention thoroughly captured, he didn't say anything more to Tayde. As soon as they all gathered around the Christmas tree, Tayde's dad began passing out the gifts. Tayde accepted the one handed to her and set it in her lap. But she didn't open it.

Knox's words repeated through her mind, and with them came guilt. Was she a hypocrite? Had she done to Gavin what had been done to her?

"Maybe the thoughts, feelings, and motivations of a perspective might carry with them an intrinsic value greater than any right or wrong."

They were the words she'd written herself the day before. Words meant to inspire others to respond in empathy and compassion to those around them, even those who'd done them wrong. And those same words convicted her now.

It's Christmas. It's Christmas. It's Christmas.

Tayde suddenly set the gift down and stood. "Excuse me. I need to go meet someone. I'll be back. Don't wait for me."

"Tayde, what are you doing?" her mom sputtered. "You can't leave. It's Christmas!"

"Exactly. It's Christmas, and there's wrong I need to get right," she said hurriedly, though she knew her mother wouldn't understand. "Someone needs to speak his story, and I need to listen."

It was already nearing noon, and Tayde knew she couldn't waste time trying to explain further. She ran out to her car and took off for downtown Brighton Falls. She hadn't taken the time to tell him she was coming, and she worried it would end as a pointless trip. After all, her last text to him had been an adamant refusal to meet him. He might not even be there when she arrived.

But desperation gripped her, and she drove anyway. Maybe he wouldn't be there to meet her, but she had to try.

Fortunately, there was no traffic on Christmas day, and she pulled to the curb by the park at two minutes before noon. Heart pounding, she jumped out of her car, her gaze anxiously scanning the cold, deserted park. He wasn't there. In fact, no one was there.

She gasped as a sob caught in her throat. Snow had fallen a

few days ago, blanketing everything with about two inches of white. Wishing for her winter boots, she walked to the middle of the park, hearing the crunch of the snow beneath her tennis shoes. She stopped in the center and turned in a slow circle as if expecting the view to change.

Maybe he was just late. Maybe he'd still come.

But in her heart, she knew it was hopeless.

She picked up her phone to see the time. She watched the numbers click to twelve o'clock.

Suddenly, she heard chiming. The sound of bells sent echoes through the air. Tayde looked around, realizing there must be a church somewhere close. The bells continued, a hollow, melodious sound filling the silent air around her.

She liked the sound and thought it nice that a church would ring the bells on Christmas day.

Can you hear the bells?

Her body jerked in recognition.

I heard the bells on Christmas Day...

That's it! That's what Bells has been referencing this entire time!

Gavin was an English major in college. He would have been familiar with the famous American poet Henry Wadsworth Longfellow. Specifically, he would have known the poet's famous poem.

Her cold, stiff fingers shook as she brought the browser up on her phone's screen. She remembered Henry Wadsworth Longfellow had written a famous poem with those words. It had even been turned into a beautiful Christmas Carol. But she couldn't remember the exact words.

She clicked on the first result, and the poem's words filled the page. Quickly, she read,

The Bells of Christmas

I heard the bells on Christmas Day
Their old, familiar carols play,
    And wild and sweet
    The words repeat
Of peace on earth, good-will to men!

And thought how, as the day had come,
The belfries of all Christendom
    Had rolled along
    The unbroken song
Of peace on earth, good-will to men!

Till ringing, singing on its way,
The world revolved from night to day,
    A voice, a chime,
    A chant sublime
Of peace on earth, good-will to men!

She kept reading as more stanzas told of the bleakness of seeing the country in the devastation of a war against itself. Then she came to a verse she felt to the depths of her whole being.

And in despair I bowed my head;
"There is no peace on earth," I said;
    "For hate is strong,
    And mocks the song
Of peace on earth, good-will to men!"

She felt Longfellow's profound grief and the utter despair that gripped him so strongly. But her breath caught and stopped as the words of the last verse rang as clearly into the world as the bells that continued to toll.

Then pealed the bells more loud and deep:
"God is not dead, nor doth He sleep;
  The Wrong shall fail,
  The Right prevail,
With peace on earth, good-will to men."

Goosebumps prickled her arms. She scrolled down from the poem and continued to read the brief backstory dating back to the nineteenth century.

Before writing the poem, Henry Wadsworth Longfellow had lost his beloved wife in a horrific accident. Her dress had caught fire while using a candle. Longfellow had tried to save her, but her injuries had proved too severe, and she passed away, leaving him with their six children. Longfellow had suffered severe burns when trying to save her and could not attend her funeral. A beard covered the burn scars on his face for the rest of his life.

Later, Longfellow's oldest son snuck away and joined the Union army in the Civil War against his father's wishes. On December 1, 1863, Longfellow received a telegram that his son had been severely injured in battle. Longfellow traveled to retrieve his son and was told that with the proximity of the bullet to the spine, his son would require a long recovery and might face permanent paralysis. Longfellow brought his son back home to nurse him back to health.

During this time, on December 25, 1863, he woke and heard the bells ringing from Cambridge, seeming to mock the current violence of the world, its injustice, and the tragedy in which his life was immersed.

He wrote the poem with the end relating a completely different outlook than the beginning. The sound of the Christmas day bells changed his perspective to one where God was still in control despite what the world appeared. God was still good. And that if he could hope in nothing else, he could hope in God—the keeper of peace and right over wrong.

Slowly, Tayde read the last verse again.

Then pealed the bells more loud and deep:
"God is not dead, nor doth He sleep;
*   The Wrong shall fail,*
*   The Right prevail,*
With peace on earth, good-will to men."

Then she looked up, hearing the Christmas day bells ringing strong and sure.

The lightbulb in her brain flickered on.

"It's a paradigm shift," she said, her voice sounding loud in the cold. A surge of excitement rushed through her.

This was what Gavin had been talking about this whole time. He'd tried to get Tayde and everyone else to "hear the bells" that would cause their perspective to change, to realize that the world was not at all what they thought.

For the very first time, Tayde heard the bells.

She took off running, trying to find the church from where the bells were ringing. They'd already been chiming for close to ten minutes, and she had no idea how much longer they'd last. Her frozen feet pounded the sidewalk, and her breath came in short puffs of visible steam in the cold air.

She ran for two blocks. The bells sounded louder, but she wasn't sure if it was just her imagination. She turned a corner, and in the distance, she saw a large stone church with a tall steeple. She kept running, and as she approached, she saw the figure of a man standing in the doorway.

Her steps slowed to a walk. She recognized him, and the

bells fell silent. Their echo vibrated through the air a few seconds before the world returned to its usual turning, with a strange void filling space that had filled with glorious sound moments before.

She reached the bottom of the long, dramatic steps leading up to the door. Her feet slowed further. She ascended the steps cautiously, wondering how he would react. Was he mad at her? She'd said no. Did he even want her here?

Then her gaze collided with his, and she felt only warmth and acceptance in his clear blue eyes. She placed her foot on the top step, and he stepped forward to meet her.

"Hi," she greeted, her feathery breath gently parting the air.

"Hi," he said. But he wasn't smiling. "You came."

There was so much she wanted to tell him. She needed to apologize and explain that she'd figured out the meaning of the bells. She opened her mouth to speak, but he shook his head before she could say a word.

"Please, Tayde. Before you say anything, let me explain."

She wanted to rush in and assure him she was here to listen. She wanted him to know she'd been wrong. But instead, she did what she should have done yesterday. She closed her mouth and waited for him to speak.

"Despite what you think, I didn't plan any of this." His tone was desperate. He wanted her to believe him, but he was clearly afraid she'd interrupt, and he'd never get to tell his side of the story. "Jarod Paulsen is my best friend. He was really upset about the letters that were written about his family, and I couldn't stand to see him mistreated, especially after everything he and the kids have been through. It reminded me of my dad and how no one took the time to look beyond the obvious to his story. I'd been helpless back then, but I couldn't watch it happen to Jarod and the kids. Like I told you before, if the column had just been ridiculous clickbait sensationalism, I wouldn't have bothered with it. But I could tell you were smart, and you were obviously a gifted writer. I responded to you with no other motive than to defend my friend's family."

Gavin paused, still seeming so upset. Tayde wanted him to continue explaining, but he needed to know she wouldn't fly off the handle if he got to a part in the story that wasn't as favorable to him. She wanted the truth but didn't want to hurt him anymore.

She nodded encouragingly. "Okay, so you didn't start with a master plan, but at some point, that changed?"

Gavin shook his head. "No, not really. I never planned to respond again after Jarod's letter. I did what I intended to do. It blew up and got a lot more attention than I ever dreamed, but it made me feel even more that I had accomplished my mission and could walk away. Then that high school girl contacted me and asked me to help her. After hearing her story, I couldn't say no, especially when I realized she needed me to be her voice so others could hear her story too. By that time, I was already fascinated by you. After you contacted me, I was completely hooked. I liked you. I liked the way you thought and wrote about things that mattered. But I also felt strongly convinced that I was speaking for those who couldn't speak for themselves. I prayed over every letter I wrote. And I prayed for you. But let me assure you, my motives weren't completely altruistic. I wanted to get to know you more, and I knew responding to one of your columns would get you to react."

"But you still used me, Gavin. You haven't gotten to that part." As a lawyer, he could be expected to talk smoothly and eloquently. And she strongly suspected that he believed every word he spoke to be true. But he also couldn't deny that his Robin Hood heroics included tricking her into investigating and reporting his father's story.

Gavin held her gaze steady. He never faltered once as he explained, "The idea never occurred to me until you wrote the letter for Knox. I recognized your writing, and I saw how you used it to tell the story you thought needed to be told. I didn't think bad of you for it. I thought it was brilliant. Every event that has happened over the past few months, every story I've heard, and every letter I've written has brought my dad's story to mind. It's been eating away at me for years. It's a helpless feeling to be able to do nothing as a child. But I was an adult—a lawyer—and I still had no hope of ever clearing his name and seeing the true villains brought to justice. I attended the gala as a guest through my firm. Russ Devoe and Sheryl Sutton never even knew my name."

"So, you knew what you were planning to do that night we met, and you never mentioned it?" Tayde asked. She could buy his innocence until then. But he could have been honest.

Gavin looked away for the first time. "I hadn't decided for sure, but the idea had occurred to me. That's why I had such a hard time deciding whether to just take my mask off and tell you who I was. But if I did, I knew I'd lose all chance of your covering the story. If you knew who I was and believed my biased version of what had happened to my dad, you'd never consent to cover it. You'd think it was a conflict of interest to write it."

"And why would it be a conflict of interest?"

His gaze came back up, and the corner of his mouth quirked up. "Personal reasons."

He sighed at Tayde's raised eyebrow, and his words came out in a rush. "Because I intended to not leave you alone. I wanted to pester you into going out with me and continue that plan indefinitely."

Tayde felt warmth spreading up her neck.

"If I even mentioned the possibility of your writing about my dad, you'd assume I was using you. I didn't want that possibility. Instead, I wanted to clarify that I am only interested in you because of you." He winced. "But I didn't exactly accomplish that, did I?"

Tayde looked down, her blush deepening at his words. "I felt like you used me," she answered quietly.

Gavin nodded, accepting her words even though his face tightened with strain. "I knew you would eventually find out who I was and that you might hate me for manipulating the situation. But you're such a gifted writer, Tayde. And I love your heart. You want to help people and right the wrongs of the world. You may have missed a few perspectives along the way, but everyone does. I trusted that if you saw a glimpse of my dad's story, you would handle it with the care that no one else has ever shown. But you wouldn't have accepted it from me. It had to be done in an anonymous letter, keeping the same pattern as always with the column. I needed you to find me before you knew my name."

"And the poem?" Tayde asked. "'Christmas Bells' by Henry Wadsworth Longfellow. I heard the bells this morning and figured it out."

Gavin smiled, and it was like the sun rising after a storm. "I knew you'd figure it out if I could get you to come down and hear them." He shrugged. "It's always been one of my favorites. I've always thought the poem described a paradigm shift—where you're living life one way, and something causes you to shift and view life completely differently. It's what the Christmas bells did for Longfellow. I've always wished someone would have 'heard the bells' for my dad. Obviously, I'm a lawyer with a wide poetic streak. At first, I wanted to ring the bells for Jarod. I hoped others would hear and experience their own paradigm shift. I wanted them to see Jarod's story differently, but I wanted it to extend to more than that. I wanted people to never again see the world the same way. I included that line, knowing no one else would understand the allusion. But it was my whole purpose. It was my goal."

It was cold enough that fine flakes of snow scuttled through the air intermittently. The slight breeze bit through Tayde's coat, and she couldn't feel her feet from her trek through the snow in the park. Tayde shivered. But as she looked up into his clear, honest eyes, there was nowhere she'd rather be.

Softly, he continued, "I'm sorry I deceived you, Tayde, but I'm not sorry about the result. You redeemed my dad and my family. Russ Devoe and Sheryl Sutton may never get legal justice, but you exposed them for what they are. Everyone knows the full story now. I want you to forgive me. I want to have you in my life. I want to talk with you and hear your perspective. But if you can't find it in your heart to forgive me, that's a cost I'm ready to pay. Because the reward you gave me is of such irreplaceable value that I can't thank you enough. I knew if I could convince you to hear the bells, you would ring them for the whole world. You rang the bells for my dad, and everyone heard."

And now she could hear the bells ringing for him. She still felt like he'd deceived her. But she didn't have to like it. She understood why he'd done it. And now the world looked different. Would she have made the same choice and written an anonymous letter to a friend, hoping he or she would cover the story?

Everything he wrote in the letter had been true to his perspective; he just didn't sign his name and didn't tell her it was his. But he hadn't forced her to follow up on the story. He hadn't forced her to write the column. He hadn't forced her to publish it.

And she didn't regret any of it. She marveled that she didn't even feel angry anymore. She recognized that events may not have transpired the same way if Gavin hadn't sent that anonymous letter.

And she kinda liked where she was right now.

She reached her hand out to his. He readily clasped it, their hands fitting together perfectly. Then she stepped just a little closer, feeling the warmth emanating from his body.

"Tayde, you need to understand I didn't plan any of this." He winced, "I'm notoriously bad at relationships, not because I didn't want something serious. I do. But I've never found someone I wanted to be serious with. Until you. I care about what you think and how you think. You fascinate me, and I want to experience life with you. I want it all—the laughter and the tears, the fun and the deep, the friendship and the love. And I want it with you. I finally *want* to do the work of a relationship. But it all came so unexpectedly."

He paused, struggling to find the words. Then he held her gaze with his and whispered, "I didn't plan to develop a public relationship with an advice columnist. I didn't anticipate she would turn out to be the most amazing woman I'd ever known. I didn't know I could clear my dad's name. I didn't predict she would use her talent and skills to redeem my family. And I had no idea that together we would change the world."

"I believe you," Tayde whispered back. "I'm sorry I didn't let you tell me your side of things yesterday. It just took me a while to hear the bells."

Gavin's gaze scanned hers hungrily, looking for confirmation of her words. Then his features relaxed. His voice trembling with excitement, he asked, "Does that mean you'll go out with me?"

Tayde smiled and nodded. "Yes, as long as we 'continue the plan indefinitely,' like you said."

"Deal," Gavin agreed. Then his gaze lost the humor, and his arms came around her to pull her close.

She went to him eagerly, loving the feel of his warm body enveloping hers. He lowered his lips to hers, pausing a mere breath above her before his lips touched hers in a gentle caress.

Tayde's heart pumped wildly, and she no longer remembered it was cold outside. His kiss was the most exquisite sensation she'd ever experienced. It was sweetness, passion, and respect all mixed into tantalizing warmth.

Then the bells started ringing... literally.

It took several seconds of the loud chimes directly overhead before Tayde came to her senses and pulled away. She looked up as the bells swayed back and forth a few more times, gradually coming back to a stop. She'd heard of music playing when a couple kissed, but church bells were a rather deafening variety.

Gavin laughed into the echo of the bells.

"That's my friend Jarod. He and his kids were in charge of ringing the church bells today. I co-opted his assignment. I guess they thought we needed an encore!"

Just when they thought the bells had stopped, they gave one last exuberant clang. Gavin looked up thoughtfully. "Actually, that one might be Jarod's girlfriend. That's something she'd do!"

Tayde laughed and leaned close, resting her head on Gavin's shoulder. She loved feeling his strong arms around her. The snow picked up its tempo, but she didn't care. She didn't want the moment to end.

It was a perfect moment. Other struggles would come, and

the bells would have to ring again for other people and other reasons. But for this one fractal of time, Tayde's arms held the evidence that wrong had failed, right prevailed, and God was definitely not sleeping.

Tayde had found her right.

Epilogue

Dear Chronicle Readers,

This letter is to thank you for your loyal readership and inform you that Chronicle Magazine no longer exists. Its assets were frozen and then used in restitution for the crimes and debts incurred by Chronicle owner Russ Devoe and editor-in-chief Sheryl Sutton. As you know, Tayde Wright's Christmas Eve column exposed Devonce Investments' fraudulent activities from fifteen years ago—crimes that could no longer be prosecuted.

However, Ms. Wright's story launched an FBI investigation in which the past fraud was discovered to have continued to current times. Some of the original evidence from Mr. Jeff Bennett was used as a map to trace forward patterns and activities that were still occurring. Both Russ Devoe and Sheryl Sutton were arrested and are currently awaiting trial for a long list of crimes. However, even the worst "villains" have their own stories, and maybe someday, these two who caused so much hurt will share theirs.

While Chronicle will no longer supply its readers with content, we are pleased to pass the torch to another venture. Many of you have followed Tayde Wright and her Wrongs Made Wright column. Tayde's column truly made us think, but it wouldn't have been the same without input from the mysterious Mr. Bells and his beautiful responses that helped us see the world from different perspectives. Tayde Wright and a few of her coworkers from Chronicle have launched their own online magazine committed to bringing readers stories that really matter from unique perspectives that show us the world from different views. This is not a sensational, clickbait-driven "rag," but a place unlike any other. If you loved Ms. Wright's column and a chance to have a voice, you'll enjoy their commitment to speaking for those who can't and right the wrongs others miss. And you'll undoubtedly see the occasional guest appearance by Mr. Bells.

Many have asked about the line with which Mr. Bells always signs his letters: "Can you hear the bells?" Ms. Wright and Mr. Bells would like to give you the opportunity to discover the meaning of the line yourself. To start your journey, they suggest you research the famous American poet Henry Wadsworth Longfellow.

After you have understood the allusion, they challenge you to find someone different than yourself, someone you don't agree with, a situation that makes you angry, an action you think is wrong, or a story that belongs to someone else. Then remember playing baseball in the graveyard, asking a nice girl to the homecoming dance, and being generous to someone who may not deserve it. Also, remember the angry student who threw a chair and the man who did wrong for the right reason of caring for his family.

And ask yourself if you can hear the bells.

May we all hear the bells, and not just on Christmas.

Personal Note

Dear Readers,

When I was young, I remember hearing the phrase, "Write what you know," and finding it very discouraging. I dreamed of being an author, but if you were required to have big, dramatic life experiences, this small-town Idaho girl was doomed. Yet, now I look back at what I've written and realize that life's small experiences can sometimes be the most valuable. *The Christmas Card* books are always my most personal, and The Bells of Christmas is no different. You will find me on every page.

Most of the stories woven through this book were inspired by my own experiences. Yes, names are changed, and details are fictionalized. The fiction version is by no means an exact replica of the real-life version, but the real one did exist. For instance, I had my gallbladder removed when I was sixteen after a four-year-long struggle with my health. I was the teenage girl waking up from anesthesia, hearing the doctor tell my mother that he didn't believe me. However, unlike Tayde, my parents believed me, and they fought until they found a doctor who did as well. I never experienced what Tayde did, but I used my own trauma from that time as inspiration for Tayde's backstory.

I was also there the day my friend found out she was terminal. Like Gavin, I never wonder what thoughts go through your mind if you find out you don't have long to live. I know. I heard them with my own ears. We sat under a sunny sky and watched our sons at a baseball practice while she unloaded every emotion possible. Now my baseball-loving friend is buried in the cemetery, and her children visit her on the Fourth of July every year. They play baseball in the open area behind the graves. My family has been blessed to share the holiday and join them for baseball and fireworks. One year, someone wrote a letter to the local newspaper and complained, never realizing the truth of the situation. I lived the real baseball in the graveyard and recognized it as a story that needed to be told.

One day, my junior high son came home and told me the true story of why a boy in his class threw a chair that day. My son and I reported what had actually happened, and the school received a call they didn't normally get. Not many advocate for a student with anger issues who misbehaves in class, but on that day, my son and I got to be the voice for someone who couldn't speak for himself.

I've bought food for someone who didn't appear to deserve it. And after the momentary shock of cigarettes and yapping dogs, I concluded that I'd do it all over again.

Yes, I was even "Nice Girl" who inadvertently hurt "Nice Guy" because of how others treated me. Unfortunately, the real story didn't have nearly the same happy ending as the book. I didn't find out until years later that Nice Guy had been sincere in his request, which still bothers me to this day.

Some details in all the stories shared in the book were exaggerated. Some were not. As to what the full truth and what the fiction is, it would probably take another entire book to sort it out. Within the over-arching tale of Tayde and Mr. Bells, every individual story but Jeff Bennett's was inspired by an actual event. Every one of them had a different perspective than the obvious. The bells needed to be rung, and people needed to hear them.

No one is perfect. I've missed hearing the bells before. I've judged unfairly. I've inadvertently been the villain to someone. I'm working on hearing the bells more often than at Christmas. This book illustrates something I continually strive to live out in my own life. I want to treat others with understanding and empathy. I watch for when God puts me in a position to be a voice for those who can't speak.

The Christmas Card books are sometimes my toughest books to write, but they are the ones God tells me to write anyway. I trust this book and its message have found you right on time. I'm praying it encourages and inspires you and that the world looks different than it did before you started. My hope for the world this Christmas and every day is that we do better at hearing the bells for each other. Our differences often seem so wide and hopeless, but even if we can't agree, the gap closes with compassion and empathy for other perspectives. If we can recognize ourselves in the faces of those who are different from us, then we can truly make the world a better place.

For all of those waiting in silence, I grabbed hold of the bells and rang them with everything in me. I hope you could hear them. Now it's your turn.

Share Your Thoughts

Dear Reader,

I hope you loved "The Bells of Christmas" and the story inspired you to hear the bells and ring them for someone else. One of the best ways to inspire the world is by sharing what inspired you. The story and message of this book will go nowhere without readers like you. Its success and impact depends on readers who share in their friend circles and by word of mouth, social media, and writing reviews.

I personally read every review on my books. I also personally respond to every email I receive from readers. I take the thoughts of readers and reviewers to heart, and I love hearing what you liked or didn't like. Knowing what you enjoy informs my writing. For instance, I'd never have written more *Christmas Card* books if they hadn't been so beloved by readers and used by the Lord to inspire so many!

Don't keep silent if you loved this book or the other books in the *Christmas Card* series. Other readers depend on reviews and friends' opinions to guide their reading time. Online retailers base much of a book's visibility on algorithms that include reviews.

Writing can be a lonely and surreal experience. I create a book that is part of myself. Then I send my "baby" out into the world to interact with people I will probably never personally meet in person. Reviews provide much needed feedback. It's how I see how God uses my work for his glory.

If this book entertained, inspired, encouraged, blessed, or caused you to see the world differently, please consider leaving a review. I will see it, and other readers will too. You are the hands, feet, and voices of "The Bells of Christmas." This book needs you to ring the bells for it, and maybe prospective readers who pass by will hear and open the cover.

I'd love to know if you could hear the bells.

```
Amazon:
     amandatru.com/cc4_amz

Book Bub:
     amandatru.com/cc4_bb

Goodreads:
     amandatru.com/cc4_goodreads
```

To leave a review, go to any link on this page and share your thoughts. I can't wait to hear from you!

Thanks!
Amanda Tru

Readers Guide

You can't see the world through someone else's eyes. Even if two people watch the same sunrise, their angle of perspective is different. It won't look the same to you as it does to me. My thoughts, feelings, emotions, knowledge, past experiences, and even what meal I ate that day all contribute to filtering the external experience into an internal one that can be processed and enjoyed. I don't see the same sunrise you see. And you can't see the same sunrise I see.

Likewise, no two people read the same book. Your experiences, emotions, knowledge, physical strengths and limitations, and past experiences filter the words of the story so that you notice different things than someone else. What is meaningful to someone else is different than what is meaningful to you. Another way of saying it is that God can use a book to meet you as an individual exactly where you are with the exact message He has for you to hear, and that message may be completely different from the message He has for someone else. Alternatively, God may use your perspective to speak to someone exactly what he or she needs to hear.

These questions are by no means exhaustive. They are only meant to get the conversation started so that you can share your perspective with each other and glean the meaning and value God has for you at this moment.

So share, listen, and speak. May our Lord inspire you to listen with empathy and compassion and speak for those who need a voice. May you ring the bells with all your heart and hear bells that once were silent.

1. *The Bells of Christmas* share numerous individual stories woven into its plot. Which story touched you the most? Which was the most startling or made you think? Which one could you relate to the most?

2. Have you ever experienced a time when you were misjudged? Tell of a time when someone thought something wrong of you and didn't understand the perspective that changed the story.
   James 4:11-12, 1 Peter 3:8-9, Psalm 34:18, Psalm 55:22

3. Did you see yourself in any of the stories? Have you ever been the "villain" and misread a situation or misjudged someone's intentions?
   Ecclesiastes 7:21-22, 1 John 1:9, 1 Timothy 1:15, Romans 7:15-20

4. It took bravery for Isaiah to go to his teacher and tell what really happened when the boy with anger issues threw the chair. Do you think this was something he needed to do, or would it have been okay to not say anything and simply pray for the boy? He could have been bullied for telling. The teacher might not have cared. How do you know when you should speak and when to let something go?
   Proverbs 31:8-9, James 4:17, Galatians 5:14, Isaiah 1:17, Ezekiel 2:1-8

5. How do you balance being generous yet also wise? Would you knowingly give food to a family who spent their money on cigarettes and pets, or do you think this encourages the wrong, unhealthy lifestyle? Should you show generosity to someone who has a lifestyle you don't agree with?
   1 Peter 4:19, John 15:12, Matthew 7:12, Matthew 9:36, Colossians 3:23-25, Matthew 6:1-34

6. Do you think you are judgmental of others? Did you find any part of this book convicting? How would you have responded if you were in any of the situations mentioned?
   Matthew 7:1-3, John 7:24, 1 Corinthians 4-5-7 Ephesians 4: 31-32

7. When talking about her brother's ex-wife, Tayde observes that "forgiving someone who'd wronged you was easier than forgiving someone who wronged someone you loved." Have you found this to be true in your own life?
   Mark 11:25, Proverbs 17:9, Provers 10:12, Colossians 3:12-13

8. When talking to Tayde, Mr. Bells says, "We can't make the world a better place unless we see ourselves in the face of others, especially those who are different from us." What does that statement mean to you? How are we supposed to view others who are different than us?
   1 Corinthians 13:12, Proverbs 10:12, Matthew 5:38

9. What was your favorite part of the book and why? What will you remember, and how will you apply it to your life?

The Christmas Card Series:
The Christmas Card
A Cinderella Christmas
Once Upon a Christmas
The Bells of Christmas

Yesterday Series:
Yesterday
The Locket
Today
The Choice
Tomorrow
The Promise
Forever
The Secret

Tru Exceptions Series:
Baggage Claim
Mirage
Point of Origin
Rogue

Crossroads Series:
Out of the Blue Bouquet
Yesterday's Mail
Under the Christmas Star
Betwixt Two Hearts
The Second Yes
When Snowflakes Never Cease
Five Gold Rings

Crossroads Companion Books:
The Random Acts of Cupid
The Night of the White Elephant

Brides by Mail Series:
(Written with Cami Wesley)
Bride of Pretense
Bride by Request
Bride of Regret

Other Christian Romance:
The Secret Bride Society
Secret Santa
The Assumption of Guilt

About Amanda Tru

Amanda is the bestselling author of more than thirty books. Her book list includes contemporary romance, historical romantic comedy, time travel, and romantic suspense.

Amanda is also the author and organizer behind the popular multiauthor Crossroads Collection series. While Amanda enjoys writing in various genres, all her books contain humor, unexpected twists, imperfect characters, and deep themes of faith. Her stories keep you turning pages and stay with you long after you shut the book.

Amanda is a former elementary school teacher who now gets to live out her lifelong dream of being an author. She lives in a small town in Idaho with her wonderful husband and four amazing children. She is an avid sports mom and loves camping, fishing, and adventuring with her family. Between her children's numerous activities and sporting events, you'll find her sneaking a few minutes of writing amidst the chaos.

Amanda sends out a monthly newsletter about her life, writing, and upcoming books. She considers her newsletter subscribers her "reader friends," and sprinkles her newsletters with humor, inspiration, and honest confessions that prove she doesn't have it all figured out. Please subscribe if you'd like to connect with Amanda and receive notifications about upcoming books!

Author site:
amandatru.com

Newsletter email sign up:
amandatru.com/trustoriesnewsletter

Facebook:
www.facebook.com/amandatru.author

Twitter:
twitter.com/TruAmanda

Pinterest:
www.pinterest.com/truamanda

Goodreads:
www.goodreads.com/author/show/5374686.Amanda_Tru

Bookbub:
www.bookbub.com/authors/amanda-trugre

Made in the USA
Columbia, SC
22 October 2024